**BradfordFranklin**

To:
Andy & Marion

From:
Jean & Bill Brown
Smyrna, TN.

Dec. 2007

i

# Fireflies
## in
# Winter

# Jack McCall

Jack McCall, CSP
PO Box 495
Hartsville, TN 37074
Phone: 615-374-3712
e-mail: jack@jackmccall.com
website: www.jackmccall.com

ISBN:0-9767676-0-0

Printed in the United States of America
First Edition

Dedicated to the memory of
my maternal grandfather
Will Herod Brim.
He made his mark.

Thanks to
Connie Martin and Doris Ward
for their efforts in typing early chapters.

Thanks to
my assistant
Florence Agee
for her creativity in
reworking the final manuscripts.

It is the writer's privilege to help
Man endure by lifting his heart.
- William Faulkner

# *Introduction*

I think that I first became enamored with an audience when I was a small boy. My maternal grandfather loved to "show me off" to any of his friends who would pay attention. A feat as simple as bending over and touching my toes was reason enough for him to exercise his bragging rights.

My first public speech was delivered when I was in junior high school. That year, six of my best buddies and I entered the seventh grade declamation contest. We memorized and recited President John F. Kennedy's first inaugural address. Quite frankly, I was the best of the seven. On contest day, the judge thought otherwise. I placed a distant 4th. After school that day I expressed my dismay to my mother. She suggested that I enter the contest again next year and win the *county* contest. She was ahead of her time. I was introduced to the concepts of "raising the bar" and "taking it to the next level" years before they became popular clichés in motivational speeches and athletic conversations.

The next year I won the Smith County declamation contest. I remember every detail of the evening, sweaty palms, nervous jitters, and, especially, *dry mouth*. I sucked lemon drops until my tongue was raw.

When I was seventeen, a crusty old Sunday School teacher made me the offer to teach his class. He allowed that his *old sawdust pile* (his mental capacity) was not what it used to be. I gave it a shot. After a few weeks, most teachers were allowing their classes to sit in on mine. It was a big auditorium type class. Almost from the beginning, I had class members ranging from 10 year old boys and girls to 85 year old men and women. The diversity of my audience forced me to become a teller of stories.

After college, I began to make the 4-H speaking circuit (Agriculture Extension Service). For making speeches, I have received paper weights, desk sets, fountain pens, framed prints, mileage and a meal, cook books, gift baskets, you name it! I would make a speech for almost **anything** of value. One of the offers that I heard most was, "We don't have any money, but we'll feed you good!" Eventually, clients actually began to pay me to make talks.

Then, in 1978, I attended The All American Rally in Nashville, Tennessee. It was a gathering of famous **motivational** speakers and trainers. On that day, a sales motivator named Zig Ziglar stole the show. I would never look at public speaking in the same way again. For the first time in my life I caught a glimpse of what I could do and possibly be.

The stories, of course, kept coming. Some, I just happened upon. Most of my best ones are ones in which I played a part. The ones that I have chosen to keep and use have a lesson tucked inside them somewhere.

A story worth passing on will always shed some light on a path, provide a flash of insight, offer a glimmer of hope, ignite one's imagination, or evoke a glowing memory. And, most often, these come at times and in places where we might least expect them . . . like *Fireflies in Winter*.

# C o n t e n t s

*Introduction*      8

*Chapter 1* Sears & Roebuck Catalog      12

*Chapter 2* The Standoff      16

*Chapter 3* Pa Rube      21

*Chapter 4* Baby Skunks      30

*Chapter 5* Hey Frank, Pass the Beans      36

*Chapter 6* Monarch Butterfly      39

*Chapter 7* GMC Trucks and a Station Wagon      44

*Chapter 8* Hauling Pigs      51

*Chapter 9* High School Basketball      63

*Chapter 10* School Bus Driver      73

*Chapter 11* Uncle Dave Manning      77

*Chapter 12* Pinto Beans, Cornbread and Sorghum Molasses      81

*Chapter 13* My Toughest Customer Ever      86

*Chapter 14* Motivational Speech      93

*Chapter 15* Choo Choo      98

*Chapter 16* Potty Training 101      103

*Chapter 17* Asian Eyes      112

*Chapter 18* The Sharecropper      116

*Chapter 19* Granny Lena and the Little Horse      121

*Chapter 20* Epilogue: On a Spring Morning      125

## *Chapter 1*

# Sears & Roebuck Catalog

On a lazy summer's morning in my 5th year my mother called me to the kitchen and announced that she had an errand for me to run by saying, "Jack, I need you to go to the store for me." The "store" was my great uncle Dewey Manning's general merchandise located three miles west of Carthage at the corner of Highway 70 and (what was then) the Old County House Road. It lay less than half a mile south of our house. You could see the back of the store building from our front porch. That was in a day when a little boy was perfectly safe alone on an isolated country road. Not only did everybody know me, but they were also looking out for me as well.

It was also a time when people were more modest than they seem to be today. As I recall, **anything** that related to certain bodily functions was hardly mentioned and if discussed at all, was done so with discretion. My mother's feminine products were well hidden under the kitchen sink and **never** acknowledged.

With some degree of boyhood resignation, I responded to her request by querying "What do you need from the store?" I froze in my tracks when she answered, "toilet paper."

"**Toilet paper! Momma, I can't.**" I objected.

She was not giving an inch. "Yes you can," she insisted, "we've got to have it."

"**Momma, I c-a-a-n't,**" I pleaded.

"Well, why not," she responded. (At least she left room for me to state my case.)

"Now, Momma, you know when I get to the store that it will be filled with people," I said flatly. "And as soon as I walk in, they will all gather around me and start teasing me and kidding me. And when I tell Uncle Dewey that I need *toilet paper*, somebody will make fun of me."

My case was presented succinctly and with passion. She considered every word carefully and thoughtfully and then she said, "If somebody makes fun of you when you ask for toilet paper, here's what you tell them." She then leaned forward and whispered in my ear as if she were sharing a secret. I thought for a moment and it sounded reasonable, I was out of the house and on the road before you could say *Jack Robinson*.

I can't recall all the thoughts that were racing through my head as I headed to the store that summer's day. I can tell you that despite my Mother's whispered advice, my heart beat began  to quicken as I got closer. I *do* remember making the last few steps that led up to the side of the store's front porch. I remember climbing on the porch and heading for the front door. My heart was in my throat as I pushed the front door open, barely enough for me to slip inside. Just as I expected, the store was filled with people. And in a moment when I wished to be invisible, every eye in the building turned and looked at me.

I tried not to make eye contact as I eased over

to the nearest set of display shelves and began to edge my way toward the sales counter. As I did, those people standing nearest to the front door began to close in behind me. I ventured further back into the store. When you are 5 years old, it's amazing how tall adults appear to be. I felt like I was being surrounded by trees. That's when it started. Someone in the gathering crowd teased, "Hey, little McCall. What are you doing in here?" Someone else added, "Hello, Jack. What brings you to town?" Still another threw in, "Why, it's one of the little McCall <u>girls</u>!" That got a chuckle or two. With my head down and my eyes glued to the floor, I managed to answer them all by weakly saying, "I've come to the store to get something  for my Momma."

By now, I had reached the counter and it seemed like everyone in that establishment was breathing down my neck. That's when my Uncle Dewey arrived on the other side, slapped the counter top with his right hand and said, "Jack, what can I do for you?" It was the moment of truth. In a whispered voice loud enough for him to hear, but low enough for the gathered masses not to, I *admitted*, "I need some ***toilet paper***."

Evidently, I did not say it low enough because as soon as the words were out of my mouth, a voice from the back of the crowd boomed out, **"Toilet paper—toilet paper, what do you mean coming to the store to buy toilet paper?"** I could feel the heat rising behind my ears.

My face flushed, but I remembered what my mother had told me. Like a steel trap snapping shut, I spun around and faced them all. I knew I had a "comeback" that just might take them all by surprise. And then, with a grin and a bit of a sneer, I said, "Y-E-A-H, we're not using the Sears and Roebuck Catalog at our house anymore."

Even I was not prepared for what happened next. Up until that day, I had never heard a room explode in laughter. It went on and on! Some of the folks were "bent double" laughing, others slapping their thighs. One man laughed until he had tears in his eyes. And then, amid all the laughter, I heard someone say, "Mary Helen put him up to that." It was true. She did. At the age of five, I had experienced "bringing the house down." That trip to the store for the embarrassing toilet paper taught me that well placed humor would lighten up almost any situation. It was a lesson that would serve me well in the years ahead.

When the laughter subsided, I tucked those four rolls under my arm and got out of there! The road back home was hot and dusty. I ran and skipped all the way!

## Chapter 2

# The Standoff

It was a banner day when my new baby brother, John, came home from the hospital. It was February, 1955. A lot of things have changed since then. Healthcare has changed. Back in those days, when a woman gave birth, she and her newborn stayed in the hospital for up to a week. She would  then come home with great fanfare for two additional weeks of bed rest. My mother was smart. When she arrived home with  my baby brother she quickly settled in to being "waited on," a welcomed change from her usual routine. But, with two small boys already in the house, she knew that her act would have to be together before she would let her feet hit the floor. Microwave ovens and pre-processed meals had not made it on the scene. We did have a dishwasher, but she was it. A full recovery and long term good health were on her mind. Getting back into her jeans was not a top priority.

And the company was comin' (translated into Southern, "the guests were arriving.") Neighbors and kinfolk seemed to come in waves. With every visitor came a special dish. I especially remember the home baked pies.

From this 4-year-old's perspective, having a new baby brother was not so bad. The food was great and it seemed like everyone was bringing the new baby a gift, and who in their right mind would not think to include me in the gift giving? After all, I was "only" 4 years old. The loot was piling up. One gift I distinctly remember was a "Fly-Back" Paddle. I can still recall in graphic detail: the bucking bronco etched on the back of the paddle, his all fours together, his back arched with the rider holding on desperately. Of course, a fly-back paddle had three moving parts–paddle, a blue-gray rubber band string, and a bright red-orange rubber ball. The object of the contraption was to bat the ball out into space and have it return to be batted again. Sustained repetition was the desired result. Quite frankly, it took skill and practice, just too much for a 4-year-old. I soon broke the rubber band and lost the bright red-orange rubber ball. I only bring this to the reader's attention because the paddle plays a role in this story later on.

So the stage is set, mother and baby, a house full of guests, and me in what my mother described as "rare form." I had never shunned an audience, so it seemed a good occasion for showing off. I was taking full advantage of the situation when my mother interceded.

I remember the first warning, "Jack, you are going to have to settle down." That warning meant that I had two more chances. (I was four, but I was smart). But, in a few short minutes, *I forgot*. Then came the second warning: "Jack, I'm telling you, you're going to have to quieten down." There was a noticeable change in her voice this time. I should have seen it coming. All went unheeded. About five minutes later came the stand off.

When it was time to really get my attention, I recall how she sat up in the bed and pointed her finger, and I remember her exact words. With fire in her eyes, through clenched teeth, she issued the challenge, "Young man, if you don't straighten up right now, I'm going to spank you!"

Now, I'm not sure how I knew that my mother was not up to 100 percent. Maybe it was the lines of pain I had noticed in her face when she negotiated herself in the bed. It could have been the fact that I had watched her struggle to get out of our pickup truck and into the house and then into the bed when she arrived home, but somehow I **knew** that she could not follow through on what she had just said.

That is why, with cool confidence, I stood my ground as I answered her challenge. Standing flat-footed, I cocked my head to one side and I sneered, "Ha, you can't get out of that bed." I promise you that is what I said.

Now, there is no way, using the words of the English language or any other language, that I can adequately portray to you the speed with which the next sequence of events took place. The words of my response had not settled in the air when suddenly my mother snatched the bed covers and flipped them over her knees and she spun out of the bed, dropping her feet to the  floor. Then, with the quickness of a cat, she sprang at me, grasping my left wrist in her left hand as she, in one fluid stroke, grabbed that fly-back paddle off the floor with her free hand. **She wasn't finished.** In what had now become a

**blur** to me, she wore the seat of my pants out with that paddle. The sound was something like machine gun fire. Then, as quickly as it had begun, the encounter was over. She let go of me, dropped the paddle, staggered backwards and sat on the bed with this funny look on her face.

*I was stunned!*

The exchange lent new meaning to the phrases, "He didn't know what hit him," and "being taken by surprise." As a thousand thoughts ran through my head, I could only manage to blurt out, "I'm going to talk to myself." And, I remember what I said to myself as I left the room, "How did she get out of that bed so fast?"

Well, the years have flown by. Not too long ago, she and I revisited that memorable day. I'm not really sure how the subject came up, but ultimately the question was poised this way. "Mother, do you remember the day when John was a baby that I told you that you couldn't get out of that bed, and you cleaned my plow?" Her reply was more animated than I anticipated. Her eyes came alive as she recalled each detail. She  said, "Honey, I looked in your eyes that day and you were so cocky I could hardly believe it; and I thought *If I let you get away with this, you'll be a "bear" to deal with next time we meet*. So I knew, not only did I have to do what I said I would do, I had to get out of the bed fast enough to catch you first, knowing that if I didn't catch you, I could not run after you."

Then she smiled a smile that was a combination

of amusement and pain, and said, "it took me **six** weeks to get over the exertion of coming out of the bed fast enough, in the condition that I was in, to catch you and deliver on my promise."

It's been 51 years now and I still haven't gotten over it. Because, you see, if there were any doubt in my mind as to whether my momma said what she meant and meant what she said, that day, she removed all doubt. From that time forward, if she said it was going to rain, I would go set the tubs out!

I'm not sure how early in life that we learn to trust. I've always believed that an unfulfilled threat is a promise broken. Through the aforementioned encounter and many others, I learned to trust my mother and my father. Consequently, I learned to place my trust in others and ultimately in God.

I think that trust is essential in building confidence in ourselves and instilling it in others. It begins with walking your talk.

# Chapter 3

# Pa Rube

A child of the 1800s, he had seen the Great Depression and the two Great Wars before I came along. He was my maternal grandfather, Will Herod Brim. His nickname was John Reuben. No one knew how that name came about; even his only daughter had no idea as to its origin. I called him "Pa Rube."

Herod Brim was the most eccentric man that I ever knew. Sensitive to a fault, he was known for wearing his feelings on his sleeve. The slightest misplacement of a word would have him pouting for a week. Some slights he <u>never</u> forgave. His superstitious nature was the stuff of legend in the community where he lived. If a rabbit or a black cat crossed the road in front of his 1951 GMC pick-up, he would turn his truck around and go back home or wear his hat backwards for a week.

He was the kind of man who was hard to get close to, and his cantankerousness kept most people at a distance. I adored him.

Pa Rube spent most his working life in the safe confines of the Brim Hollow. Purchased in 1835 by his great grandfather, John Brim, it was a hollow in the truest sense of the word. Two ridges ran the length of the farm on the east and west sides and converged to form a horseshoe in the "head" of the hollow. Brim Hollow provided the setting in which I would spend the most carefree days of my life.

One can never know how much time one has. When you are a growing boy, you just drink it all in. How could I ever have known that my window of opportunity was a limited one?

It began in my sixth year. That's when I first started spending weeks at a time with my Pa Rube and Granny Lena in the Brim Hollow.

There was never a dull moment. The home place was without running water or indoor plumbing. Electricity was limited to one 220 outlet for the electric oven, which my grandmother used sparingly in the summer. (She preferred her woodstove). Drop cords with light bulbs on the ends provided lights in most rooms. The only source of heat outside the kitchen was a fireplace in the central bedroom. I slept in the bedroom on the opposite side of the fireplace where there was no heat. In the winter time you could see your breath when you entered that bedroom. To save me from frostbite, my  grandmother would take a woolen pillow case and hold it up in front of the fire until it was smoking. Then she would say, "Let's go." She'd throw open the bedroom door and I would *fly* to  the featherbed and dive in. She would be following in hot pursuit. As she held up the warm pillowcase, I would slide my feet inside. It was toasty warm. She then crawled in the bed behind me and we backed up to each other while pulling 27 pounds of quilts over our heads. We wouldn't move while we waited for the bed to "warm up." There was no better feeling in the world. Well, maybe there was one. That would be lying in that same bed on a spring night and listening to a gentle rain falling on the tin roof overhead. Life could not have been any better.

Summer days were spent gathering eggs, picking blackberries, bringing vegetables in out of the garden, drawing water from the well, feeding the baby chicks, and doing all the other activities involved in running a country household. Of course, there was plenty of time for play. The hollow provided a perfect setting for a growing boy to use his imagination. I was into cowboys and indians. One day I would be Roy Rogers, and the next day I would be Gene Autrey. I had one stick horse that ran down more outlaws and outran more Cheyenne war parties than any pony that ever raced across the western frontier.

I found a perfect place to build hideouts among the towering weeds in the edge of the  yard. That was the same place where the laying hens would weave tunnels in and out. It was wise to watch where you placed your hand while crawling down a chicken path. That's where this cowboy learned that there were two kinds of chicken droppings. One was two-toned, gray and white, and had a chalky texture and was virtually odorless. The other was black. You **did not** want to get into that black stuff. It looked like licorice gel toothpaste and had a smell that would follow you around all day. It was cause for many a barefooted cowboy having to have a foot bath and wash between his toes before crawling between clean white sheets at bedtime.

Of course, the outhouse was a special curiosity to an adventurous boy. It was located inconspicuously behind the hen house. To get there from the house, one had to follow a path that led by the smokehouse, then cross a two log footbridge across a dry branch (that was my grandmother's favorite word for a little creek), then circle around behind the henhouse.

One rarely made a trip to the outhouse after dark. If someone had to go, it meant firing up the coal oil lantern. Generally, the chamber pot was used after dark. My grandmother called it the "slop jar." Fortunately, it came equipped with a lid.

The outhouse was a standard "one holer." A sign of prosperity in those days was a "two holer," which brought to my mind a question. "Who would *you* want to sit with?" The Brim hollow "one holer" was meagerly appointed. A calendar graced one wall. I noticed that it was never the correct year. Pa Rube insisted on saving calendars. He pointed out that each one would be good again in seven years. There was also a book of instruction on the art of tying knots. I think it was titled, ***How to Tie a Knot***. I speculated that Pa Rube practiced his knot tying while he was waiting for time to pass in the outhouse. And, of course, there was last year's Sears and Roebuck Catalog. It was always lying on the outhouse seat easily within arms reach. I was quick to notice that the index pages always disappeared first. My grandfather was known to carry a couple of index pages triple folded in his pocket. Seems the wear and tear of being toted around made index pages even softer. Those pages came in mighty handy when one was caught out in the woods without a source of bathroom paper.

Pa Rube was well known in the Riddleton Community. Everyone either knew him or knew *of* him. The entrance to the Brim Hollow was less than a mile from downtown Riddleton. Like many communities of that era, downtown amounted to two general stores. Gilmer Brimm's store served as the Riddleton Post Office. Leonard Carter's General Merchandise, the larger of the two, was my grandfather's favorite hangout.

For all of the years that I knew him, Pa Rube spent some time everyday whittling cedar on the front porch of Leonard Carter's store. When the morning sun got high enough, he and his cronies would move across the street and spend the rest of the day in the shade. Whittling and talking, talking and whittling, comparing pocket knives, **trading** pocket knives. The telling of tales went on and on. At the end of the day, cedar shavings would be piled up almost to their knees. How he could enjoy that routine day after day still baffles me to this day. It was just a slower time.

I have been told that my grandfather could sit at the store all day and never eat a bite of food or take a drink of water. As far as I know, he never purchased a soft drink for himself. In the

Riddleton Community he was known for being "as tight as the bark on a tree."

He had peculiar eating habits too! He ate two hardboiled eggs at every meal. When my grandmother placed the eggs on his plate, he would begin his ritual. He would finely chop the eggs with his fork, add an exact amount of butter and salad dressing, then lots of salt and pepper. Then, he would chop the entire mixture again. I saw him do it hundreds of times, never any variation in his routine. With his eggs, he always ate crispy dry toast or saltine crackers. He **loved** saltine crackers. Occasionally he would break down and buy a box. It was only one of two purchases that I ever saw him make. It was the other purchase that would create a lifetime of memories for me.

My weeklong stays in the hollow always began the same way. My entire family would load up in  the pickup truck after church on Sunday, and we would make the fifteen mile trip across the county. To a boy, fifteen miles seemed like forever. We would spend Sunday afternoon "visiting" and at days end, everybody packed up to head back home. It was usually prearranged that I would stay behind to spend the following week. In my mind's eye, I can still see our pickup truck as it headed out of the hollow leaving me behind. The first few times, that experience left me feeling a little bit lonely. Actually, I wanted to cry, but I never let on. As I got older, my excitement only grew as I watched that truck go out of sight.

Pa Rube would announce early on Monday

morning that we were going to the store. I knew what was coming. Just he and I made this trip. When we arrived at Leonard Carter's store, he led the way as we went inside. In a booming voice he would say, "Good morning, Lent." I could *hear* the pride in his voice. Then he would order six Nehi sodas, three orange and three grape, and six "Hersey" bars. He always mispronounced Hershey by leaving out the second "H." At my suggestion, he ordered three plain and three with almonds. He would count out the money and we would be on our way. When we got back to the house, I would line the Nehis up in the refrigerator door–orange, grape, orange, grape, orange, grape. Counting Monday, I was set for the next six days. Some nights I would lie awake in that feather bed daydreaming about "tomorrow." The question was: When will I eat my Hershey bar and drink my Nehi tomorrow? Most mornings after an early breakfast, I would wash the Hershey bar down with a glass of cold milk somewhere around 10:00 a.m. In the afternoon, when I was playing cowboy, I would drink that Nehi out of a shot glass. I promise  you, when you've been out on the trail all day, wouldn't anything cut that trail dust out of your throat like a shot of grape Nehi. When you slugged that stuff, that carbonation burned all the way to the bottom.

That was many years ago, but I have memories that are tied to those Nehis and Hershey bars that make the events seem as only yesterday.

To this very day, on occasion when I'm driving on a rural road and see any resemblance of a country store, I'll stop my car. Then I'll go inside and approach the counter and say, "Give me a Nehi and a Hershey bar." Nehis are getting harder to come by. Sometimes I have to substitute a Welch's Grape or a Sunkist Orange. I'll go outside and find a cane bottomed chair, wooden bench or an old rocking chair, and I'll sit down and take a trip (in my mind). In a moment, I am ten years old again, and "Old Skip" and I are hunting groundhogs as I carry Pa Rube's favorite 22 caliber rifle, bolt action, single shot with a peep sight, or I'm exploring some narrow path in short britches careful to watch for stinging weeds. One day I got bored and told Pa Rube that I didn't have anything to do. That was a mistake! In my grandfather's work room, he kept three, one-gallon buckets filled with crooked, rusted nails, steeples, washers, bolts, you name it. He handed me one of the buckets  and instructed me to count out 25 or 30 of the crooked nails. Then he gave me a tack hammer and had me straighten the nails by hammering them against a flat rock. When I finished that, he told me to drive the newly straightened nails into a stump that sat close by the shed. That ordeal took up half a day. I never said I was bored again!

Those days were like the ones described in the lyrics of the song "Summertime,"—"where the livin is easy." Slipping back to those days of yesteryear has always been galvanizing to me.

When I finish off the Hershey bar and discard the soda bottle, I'm always **better** for having made the trip across the miles.

Someone has said, "recall a great memory as often as you like. You can never wear it out."

Psychologists say that it is therapeutic to recall the best events from your past. Those great moments of your life when you won the prize, or you did the right thing, or you came through, or you loved someone and/or they loved you. Only you can relive your moments. It is called drawing on the equity of your life. It is for your good. It will feed your soul.

# Chapter 4
# Baby Skunks

For most of my father's life he farmed a part of the old Manning farm that had been willed to my grandmother by her father, Burr Manning. The Cumberland River formed the northern boundary of the farm. Our house was built on top of a hill where the original Manning homestead had burned to the ground many years past. The river bottom presented a panoramic view from the window over my mother's kitchen sink. I spent more hours in that river bottom than I care to remember, most of them hauling hay and chopping Johnson Grass.

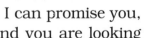

It's amazing how agriculture has changed since those days. I have taken note with special interest in the evolution of pesticides: Sevin, Toxiphene, Malythion, Dyasinon, and Dursban, to name a few. Under the category of herbicides: Roundup, Lasso, Panther, Pounce, Crossbow, Classic, and Scepter are some popular names that have come and gone. In my boyhood days, however, we only had two things for controlling insects and weeds: DDT and H-O-E! DDT has been banned because it presents a health hazard. But, I can promise you, when you are ten years old, and you are looking down a corn row that looks to be a half mile long, and it's 97 degrees in the shade, and the sweat bees have chosen you as food of the day, that hoe presents a health hazard as well.

The road to the river bottom circled down by the main feed barn and then through the back cow lot where it ended in a flat rock creek bed at what we called the bottom gate. The creek was fed by a spring that ran year round, located several hundred yards up the fence row. Run-off from rainfall coupled with the flow of the spring supplied the creek bed with an abundance of silt. To put it another way, the creek bed was always muddy. When we worked down in the river bottom, my brothers and I were the designated gate openers. That muddy creek bed and the gate to the river bottom provided a perfect set-up for one of my father's favorite pranks.

After a long day of chopping corn or hauling hay that bottom gate became a welcomed sight. It came to symbolize the end of the day. By the time we arrived there, bodies were tired and sometimes tempers were short. The gate opener for the day was usually pre-designated by some kind of primitive pecking order. Just before someone had to climb out of the truck to get it, a chorus of complaints could be heard. It would go something like this: "It's your turn," "I got it last time," "If you don't get it, you'll walk to the house," "Daddy, make him get the gate." It could go on and on.

Finally one brother would relent and begin the task of pushing the gate open. The challenge was in supporting the weight of the gate while negotiating the ever present build-up of mud in the creek. It was always a bit of a struggle.

As my father drove through the gate, the rear

axle of the truck would come to rest in the center of the creek bed and the stage was set! In order to shut the gate, the gate opener had to pass directly behind the truck. When he came in direct line with the rear wheel that had positive traction, my father would be waiting. That's when my father in a rascally playful mood would pop the clutch and pour on the gas. The tire would spin and mud would fly. Daddy never failed to get a good laugh from this.

I got it more than once. The first time I had mud on me from the heels of my shoes, up the back of my legs and up the back of my baseball cap. In my mind's eye, I can still see my father's laughing face in the trunk rearview mirror. Of course, after a few times, you got wise to it. You certainly learned to watch that rearview mirror. Then it became fun to help set the younger brothers up. It was a kind of baptism at the bottom gate.

My father's boyish prank brought a light-hearted respite to what had been a long day and put a little spark into an otherwise boring routine.

But nothing he ever did compared to the day he brought home the skunks.

We knew something was up the afternoon we heard him laying on the truck horn as he made his way up the gravel road to our house. Of course, all four of us boys came out to see what was going on. He parked the truck at the side of the house and climbed out of the cab with a funny kind of grin on his face. He then quickly stepped to the back of the truck and, with some effort, pulled a large cardboard box out of the truck bed. When I say a large box, I mean one big enough for a washer or a dryer or a console television set. He set the box on the ground with his face beaming and said, "Come here boys and see what I found." We all gathered around the box and peered inside. In the bottom of the box, cowering in the corner furthest from us, were two of the cutest baby skunks that I had ever seen. They were literally little black and white striped fur balls with tiny intense black eyes, and they were horrified.

My father still had that funny grin on his face as he challenged, "Get over in there and play with them." By now, my mother, having heard the commotion, had arrived. From somewhere behind me I heard her warn, "Boys, I don't think I would do that if I were you."

My Dad continued, "Ah, they're too little to spray you. Get over in there and play with them."

On that day, I was the bravest of the four (or the dumbest) so I began to lean over in the box in a taunting fashion like boys will do. Nothing seemed to be happening at first, so I gradually gathered my nerve and began to lean further over into the box. That's when my father handed me a stick.

I reckon that I was almost upside down and about up to my waist in that box, with my face no more than two feet from the nearest skunk when that little critter did the quickest about-face that I will ever witness. I can still remember with exceptional clarity the sound of his little claws scratching the bottom of that cardboard box as he attempted to "set" his feet in order to deliver his "goods." With stunning accuracy he sprayed me up the entire left side of my upper body, in my left eye, and in my hair. OBSERVATION: At point blank range a skunk does not smell like skunk!

The stuff one smells when a skunk has been run over on the highway, that's not **pure** skunk. That's **diluted** skunk! At close range, skunk doesn't smell at all. **It burns**! That stuff is pure ammonia!

I now know personally why skunk is not very high on the predator food chain. I have seen dogs go crazy after being sprayed by a skunk. I have seen some howl pitifully, others drop their chins to the ground and with their hind legs push themselves through the grass on their bellies. I have seen others cover their eyes and ears with their paws and moan and whine helplessly. I understand why.

I don't remember **anything** that happened immediately after that little critter let me have it! I do know that I couldn't see very well out of my left eye for a day or two. The hair on the left side of my head turned **green**. I do remember my mother pouring Clorox bleach in my bath water. For whatever reason, she kept the shirt that I was wearing that day. I remember the shirt. It was orange. Years later, whenever she ironed that shirt, she confessed that she could still pick up the slightest trace of skunk smell.

I'm sure my father got a kick out of my "misfortune" that day. It's funny to me, now.

As I look back across the years, I think of how my father's playful disposition blessed our lives so many times and in so many ways. Strangely, I never felt victimized.

It was just another experience in being part of a big happy family.

## *Chapter 5*

# Hey Frank, Pass the Beans

I grew up in a time and place where the phrases "yes ma'am," "no ma'am," "yes sir," "no sir," "please," "thank you" and "you're welcome" were standard operating procedure. Furthermore, if it was remotely suspected that someone was your senior, they were referred to with Mr. or Mrs. (we usually said "Miss") as a prefix to their name.  Some of the men and women that I respected most in my boyhood days were people I called Mr. Reece, Mr. Marvin, Mr. Sam A., Mr. Robert L., Mr. Charlie, Miss Johnnie Mae, Miss Beatrice, Miss Vergie Mae, and Miss Eunice. Last names were rarely used. Everybody knew who you were  talking about. And, we **never** called our father or mother by their first name.

Well, maybe once.

I can still remember the night at the supper table when my youngest brother, Dewey, decided to try his wings. With a boyish nonchalance, he turned to my father who always sat at the head of the table, and barked, "Hey Frank, pass the beans."

I wish you could have seen the bugged eyes around the table. The older brothers looked at each other in disbelief. We, then, all waited for what was coming. We were not sure **what** was coming, but we all knew **something** was fixing to happen.

I must digress for a moment to enlighten the reader as to the tremendous strength that my father had in his forearms. The workhorse of our farming operation in those days was a 1941 Model A, John Deere tractor. Some people called that particular series of tractor Poppin' Johns. In the Mid-West, they call them Johnnie Poppers. For whatever reason, my father removed the electric starter soon after it was purchased. Therefore, in most situations, he started the tractor by hand. It literally involved his grasping the tractor flywheel and turning the tractor engine over with his "bare hands." It required exceptional strength. My father had exceptional forearms.

Well, when my brother Dewey said, "Hey, Frank, pass the beans," my brother, John, who was sitting between them, leaned hard against the back of his chair. He wasn't sure what was going to happen but he was sure he didn't want to be in the line of fire. As he did, my father reached for my brother Dewey, and for a fraction of a second allowed his hand to hover just over my little brother's head. Then, he turned his hand with his thumb pointing downward and formed a pair of vise-grip pliers with his thumb and forefinger. With that he gathered up all the hair that he could grasp on the top of Dewey's head and straight-armed him out of his seat. He stared straight into Dewey's eyes for a split second; then he let him go.

Now, in the house where I grew up, that was called *communication*. Message delivered.

Message received. There was nothing lost in the communication. Was it effective? Absolutely!

About two weeks later we were all seated at the same table. Only this time, a boy from the neighborhood was our supper guest. As introductions were being made, our guest turned to Dewey and asked, "what's your father's name?" I can still hear Dewey as he whispered his answer, through cupped hands, into the boy's nearest ear, *"His name is Frank, but don't call him that, 'cause he'll pull your hair!"*

I know we live in an age where some would call my father's teaching technique child abuse. I would argue that it was the furthest thing from it. My father's intentions were not to **hurt** my brother but to **instruct** him. In this particular incident, to give him something to **think** about the next time he considered calling him "Frank." In this case it was **pain**. The overriding issue was **respect** for our father's authority. I have no doubts that he knew what he was doing. Each of his children respected him and loved him until the day he died.

## Chapter 6

# Monarch Butterfly

It was one of those fall days that one dreams about. The temperature was perfect, the sky was clear and the wind was playing just enough to let us know that cold weather was on its way. I was helping "gather" corn in the autumn of my ninth year.

Not many mechanical corn pickers had made their way onto the small farms in the south in those days. So, when I say "gathering" corn, I mean that we were "hand picking" corn. My father would go to the cornfield ahead of time and "pull" the rows that the tractor and wagon would knock down as we passed through the field. He would neatly pitch the ears of corn into piles every 20 or 30 feet. He and a neighbor or  two would then pick four rows on each side of the wagon as we worked our way from one end of the cornfield to the other.

My job entailed picking up the "down row" (the piles of corn) and driving the tractor. This involved starting the engine, pulling the wagon  up 20 or 30 feet, climbing off the tractor, pitching my corn into the wagon, and climbing on the tractor again.

If I worked quickly, I could create a little period of "resting" time to sit on the tractor and daydream while I waited for the pickers to catch-up. I took one of these brief respites to glory in the absolute wonder of that incredible fall day. I turned around in the tractor seat, which felt a bit awkward, and let my legs dangle as I surveyed the glory of that fall day. The sky was deliciously blue. Against its back-drop, all the earth tones of fall and the camel-colored corn were comforting to the eye. I remember the red of the tractor picked up in my lower peripheral vision. With a restful kind of pleasure my eyes focused from earth to sky and back again.

Then I saw it.

In contrast to the golden corn, its dazzling jade color was riveting though it was incredibly tiny from so far away. Afraid that I would lose sight of it in the wave of corn blades, which  flowed lazily with the wind, I refused to break eye contact. I slid over the back of the tractor seat and dropped to the ground narrowly missing the wagon tongue. Then, using my hands, I felt my way along the sides of the wagon as a blind man would grope for direction. As I left the back of the  wagon, I stumbled through the corn until I arrived at the focus of my curiosity. There it was, attached to the underside of a blade of corn located near the top of the stalk. It was no larger than the first joint of a man's finger, and it was the most beautiful silken jade color that I had seen in all my nine years. It was inanimate, but it spoke of life. On its surface, flawless symmetrical swirls flowed either to or from a beautiful orange eye that refused to blink.

My science class had recently completed a study of moths and butterflies. In that study we had learned about cocoons and chrysalises. I had found a chrysalis, the stage between a caterpillar and a butterfly!

I carefully detached my newfound treasure and placed it tenderly in my cap, turned upside down to form a cradle, and returned to the tractor to place the cap and treasure safely in a resting place between the gearshift and the tractor instrument panel. As the day wound down, I checked in on my new "friend" with regularity. I could hardly wait to get to school on the following day. I would be the star of "show and tell." Sleep did not come quickly that night.

The next morning my discovery proved to be a big hit in the classroom. Everyone was oooing and ahhing. When Mrs. Hailey, my 4th grade teacher, saw the object of our attention her enthusiasm was unbounding. She placed the insides of her hands to her checks and said, "Oh my goodness, I'll bet there's a monarch butterfly inside." A monarch butterfly. I had seen those big orange and black butterflies before, but I had never attached a name to them. A monarch butterfly. I could not imagine one of those big, beautiful butterflies emerging from that small fragile chrysalis that I had found!

Mrs. Hailey exclaimed, "Let's put it up in a safe place and see if a monarch butterfly comes out in the spring." I noted how she emphasized the word *spring* as she gently lowered the precious jade capsule into a paper clip box and placed it safely in a place of honor on a bookshelf.

As fall days flew by, I checked in on our sleeping friend regularly. Of course, he had not so much as moved. Then, the Thanksgiving holiday sent us home for an extended weekend.

On the first Monday after Thanksgiving, I entered the classroom that morning with that monarch chrysalis on my mind. I went to the shelf, took down the box, opened it carefully, and looked inside. I was expecting my eyes to immediately focus on the small jade chrysalis, but instead of seeing jade, I saw orange—lots of orange—a box filled with orange.

It took a moment for the reality of the moment to sink in. My magnificent monarch butterfly, fooled by the temperature of the room into sensing that it was spring, had emerged prematurely to find himself in what ultimately proved to be its coffin. His beautiful wings were folded and frayed from his struggle against the confines of the box. I shuttered at the thought of how long he may have fought before he gave up.

Forty-five years have passed and as I recall this scene, I have the same sick feeling in my stomach that I felt that day. My magnificent butterfly would never spread his glorious wings and fly because he had been put in a box! My intervention into his life cycle had led to his ruin. I took little consolation in the thought that if left in the cornfield he would have ultimately been disked underground after the corn was harvested. But now, years later, I have taken consolation in the lesson that he taught me.

In my lifetime I have seen lots of boxes, lots

and lots of different kinds of boxes. Inside those boxes I have seen lots of people. Sometimes I've found myself in a box.

Some of the boxes were constructed with walls of fear, or guilt, or "might have beens." Some were fashioned by limiting voices of the past, others by negative self-talk. Some were real, but most imagined. Some were temporary; others were permanent but didn't have to be. All were confining.

I wince when I consider the millions of lives that never made it off the ground because of boxes. Folded wings meant to fly that were never spread. Wings that never felt the lift of the wind or the glorious feeling that only soaring brings.

Ever found yourself in a box? Are the walls real or imagined? My monarch butterfly had no choice in the matter. But you have choices to make.

What is holding *you* back?

## *Chapter 7*

# GMC Trucks and a Station Wagon

Our father purchased our first automobile in the fall of 1961. Prior to that time our family did all its traveling in the farm pick-up truck. My father was a GMC man. Before he was through, he would own new ones in 1948, 1958, 1968, and 1978. I knew the world was changing when he started buying Toyotas. His GMC's never had a conventional metal bed. He built his own flat bed onto which he constructed a "cattle rack." There was not another like it in our part of the country.

After our sister came along, things got crowded in the cab of our pick-up. My mother teased that we packed ourselves in that truck like **sardines**. Summertime was not so bad because my brothers and I were allowed to ride in the back of the truck. The rules were hard and fast. No riding near the back and you could only climb three slats high on the front of the truck bed. That would put your head and shoulders above the top of the rack.

For a boy, riding in the back of a truck was something special, the wind in your hair, the sun on your face. Facing straight ahead into the wind would almost take your breath.

I know what a windshield feels like. I've hit a June bug head on at 55 miles per hour. To keep the gnats from getting in our eyes we tried riding with our mouths open. One day I swallowed a stink bug. They taste just exactly like they smell. And those yellow bugs? I'm not sure what color they are on the outside. I just know when they hit a windshield, they are **yellow**. One day I was riding on the left side and my brother John was riding on the right. The truck had just reached cruising speed when I heard him moan "oooooohh." I turned quickly to witness his distress; **yellow bug**. He had taken a hit right smack in the middle of his forehead. It looked like he had been painted with a yellow highlighter.

Winter time presented a special challenge. It was too cold to ride in the back and winter coats made everyone even bulkier. Through trial and error, we got cramming us all into the cab of the truck down to a science. My mother declared that it was like putting a jigsaw puzzle together. If one piece got out of place we had to get out of the truck and start all over. Eventually we approached it with workmanlike precision.

Here's how it worked. First, my father would get in and **lock** his door. That was important! He would then scoot against the driver side door. Next, my bother Dewey would climb in through the passenger door and sit on the front edge of the seat against my father's right knee. My mother then got in and sat next to my father and behind Dewey with her legs turned to the right. That created a spot for my brother John to stand up against my mother. Next, I climbed in and sat on the front edge of the seat against my mother's knees. My brother, Tom, now had barely enough room to get in the truck. At this moment we all leaned hard toward my father as Tom tried to close the passenger door. (In case you are wondering my sister is in my mother's lap.) Sometimes it took three attempts to get the door shut and locked. One evening as we were getting ready for bed I noticed a big ugly bruise on Tom's right hip. I asked, "What happened?" He matter-of-factly answered, "It's that door handle." I realized what a tight fit the truck ride had become.

But all that changed in the fall of 1961. My father waited until the 1962 models were introduced and went in search of a bargain. He found the one that he was looking for at Jim Reed Chevrolet in Nashville. It was a 1961 Chevrolet Parkwood station wagon, white with red interior. He paid cash for it. It was the only way he did business. As I recall, the price was $2,600.00, taxes included. We all loaded up in the pick-up and drove to Nashville to pick it up. That day my mother and sister came back in the truck. The "boys" brought home what we would in later years affectionately refer to as the "snowgoose." That white station wagon was an instant hit. It had a three-speed manual shift on the steering column and was equipped with a dropdown rear tailgate complete with a power window. We especially liked the third seat which faced the rear. That third seat was a great place to be. We found out immediately that our father could not reach us from the front seat. In a strange way that car opened up a new world for our family. Among other things, it made it possible for us to take our first family vacation.

That took place in the summer of 1962. That year my father purchased our first camping tent. It was a 12 x 12 heavy tarpaulin shelter complete with an elaborate aluminum framework—hard to handle, but perfect for the great outdoors. We quickly set about making plans to spend a week camping in the Great Smokey Mountains National Park. Since my sister was just past her first birthday, the plan was to leave her with my Uncle Ray and Aunt Helen in Cookeville, Tennessee. My Uncle Ray pastored a church there. As a fair exchange, we would take my cousin, Ray McCall, Jr., on the camping trip with us. With our new station wagon we had plenty of room, and with a car full of boys, the more the merrier.

Ray McCall, Jr. will always be listed among my most unforgettable characters. It seems like from the beginning he had more than one strike against him. First, he had the suffocating burden  of being a preacher's kid. Add to that the fact that he was a "city" boy. Then, to make things more challenging, he was dropped "in between" two sisters. When he visited his cousins in the summer he would try things that country boys knew to leave alone—like jumping out of barn bonnets and trying to ride 600-pound bull calves in stables with low ceilings. My brothers and I really loved him (and still do). We were excited to have him on our first vacation.

On a July morning we dropped my sister off in

Cookeville and headed out on I-40 East. It did not take long for five boys wide-eyed with excitement to start bouncing all over that station wagon. Just a few miles up the road and the three in the middle seat began to get territorial. Each was laying claim to his section of the seat. My mother intervened by instructing each boy to stay on his third of the seat. That wasn't good enough. I heard someone complain, "Mama, he's looking at me!" I promise that I heard her say, "Don't look at your brother!" That wasn't good enough either. Then, the offended said, "Mama, he's smiling." And, she said, "You stop smiling right now!"

At this point, one of the boys in the back thought it a good idea to join the three in the middle seat. So, he climbed over. That's when my father said, "I don't want to have to stop this car!"

My father never was one to make idle threats. Upon the sound of his voice, the climber deftly retraced his route over the back of that seat. All was peaceful again for a moment. Then someone on the second seat yelled out, "Daddy, somebody thumped my ear!"

My father checked the traffic behind him through the rearview mirror; then he hit the breaks hard. He eased our car off the interstate onto the shoulder of the road and brought it to a complete stop. With a voice stern, but calm he instructed us to line up on the side of the car opposite the traffic. Then he said, "I'll be right back." With that said he started walking toward

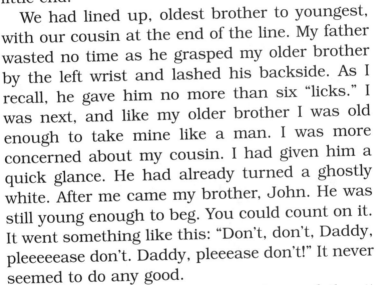

the tree line which lay at least fifty feet away. He approached a tree of his liking, retrieved his pocket knife, and with one stroke cut a wicked looking limb off the tree. (I say wicked looking. It could not have been bigger that a man's thumb at the large end of the limb. But from where I was standing, it looked wicked to me.) As he turned in our direction, he began to strip the leaves off the limb starting at the big end. By the time he reached us, only a few leaves remained at the little end.

We had lined up, oldest brother to youngest, with our cousin at the end of the line. My father wasted no time as he grasped my older brother by the left wrist and lashed his backside. As I recall, he gave him no more than six "licks." I was next, and like my older brother I was old enough to take mine like a man. I was more  concerned about my cousin. I had given him a quick glance. He had already turned a ghostly white. After me came my brother, John. He was still young enough to beg. You could count on it. It went something like this: "Don't, don't, Daddy, pleeeeease don't. Daddy, pleeease don't!" It never seemed to do any good.

If I had only one word to describe my father it would be the word "reasonable." I even observed it in how he administered discipline. I noted with satisfaction that as the boy got smaller, the number of "licks" were fewer and the weight of the switch was lighter. Dewey, the youngest of my brothers was a dancer. He always danced as he took his "medicine." I guess he thought it wouldn't hurt as bad if he was moving. I checked on my cousin again. As my father finished with Dewey, my cousin's face took on the look of a man who was staring straight into the eyes of death. I wondered how my father would handle this boy who was not his. As he released Dewey's hand, he turned and faced my cousin squarely and in a stern voice he said, "And I'd better not hear anything else out of you, either."

My cousin had been spared. My father had chosen not to a lay a hand on his brother's son, but I noted that a certain kind of justice had been served him as well. As we began to get back into the car, I observed that Ray McCall, Jr. had wet his britches.

# Chapter 8
## Hauling Pigs

One of the jobs that fell to me during my high school days was hauling my grandfather McCall's feeder pigs to market. Known to the McCall family as "Pa Dave," my grandfather was well known for his physical toughness and especially his shrewdness as a businessman. He could spot a good "deal" from a mile away. My father, the only farmer among my grandfather's five sons, was prone to accommodate his father whenever he could. Even though Pa Dave had his own truck he was inclined to call my father when he had pigs ready for market.

The fact that my father drove a school bus made it necessary for one of our farm vehicles to make a trip to town five mornings a week. Pa Dave saw that as an opportunity for his feeder pigs to hitch a ride to town on feeder pig sale day—which fell on Thursday—at little or no cost to him. This is how it worked.

Pa Dave would call our house early on a Thursday morning. My mother would answer the phone. After exchanging greetings, he would ask, "Where's Frank?"

"He's right here," my mother would respond.

"Let me talk to him," he would say.

"Alright," my father would say when handed the phone.

"Frank, can one of your boys haul my pigs to the pig sale this morning?"

My father always complied with his request. For the two of them it was actually a win-win situation. My grandfather got his pigs hauled, and my father did something that appeased his father without getting involved. That's where I enter the picture.

The pig hauling duties naturally fell to me. I was the only son at home who had a driver's license, and I usually drove the truck to town each morning. I had reason to protest on a number of fronts.

First, (and it was because of his generation) my grandfather had no concept of what a "feeder pig" was. To him, if it was a hog and it could still eat, it was a feeder pig. A true feeder pig was marketed at an average weight of 45-47 lbs., meaning that the normal weight range was between 35 and 65 lbs. Pa Dave's pigs could weigh from 30 lbs. to 130 lbs. And, hauling them was not limited to just hauling them. It meant *catching* them first. He usually had them corralled in the stable at the far end of the feed barn. They had been "put up" the night before which meant that their legs would be covered  with fresh, black stable manure. That fact alone created special problems for the pig catcher.

 Loading them entailed grabbing a pig by its hind leg (or legs depending on the size of the pig), dragging it out of the stable while Pa Dave held the stable door open, wrestling it down the length of the barn hallway, and then hoisting it up into the back of the truck. Working a big pig was no small undertaking. You had to grasp them by both back legs (one in each hand) and literally drag them to the truck. All the while the pig was still standing on his front legs and digging in for all he was worth. I've had them jerk their back legs back and forth so hard that my teeth chattered. Hauling pigs for Pa Dave was a physically demanding ordeal.

Secondly, there was the issue of payment for services rendered. My father was one of the easiest-going souls that one could ever meet. And for some reason he found it difficult to charge Pa Dave for any work that he did for him. We could never seem to agree on a fair price to charge Pa Dave for my hauling his pigs. My father wanted me to be paid, and he agreed that it was only right and fair that I be compensated for my efforts. But, when the question "What do I charge him?" came up, the answer was always the same. My father would say, "Ahh, just ask for enough to cover the gas and get yourself a little spending money." That meant two or three dollars, maybe four at the most.

The third issue was one known to all hog farmers, **the smell**. Of all the manure produced  by farm animals, nothing competes with that which a hog leaves behind. The smell of hogs is legendary. You don't have to step *in* it to get it *on* you. The odor *clings*. You can go *near* hogs and come away smelling *like* them. The dilemma was heightened for me because I was a high school age boy who was seriously interested in high school age girls. There was neither time nor place  for me to shower and change clothes after loading and delivering the pigs. That which I wore to the barn that morning would be my clothes for the day. I tried everything to insulate myself from the smell. I wore coveralls, overshoes, and leather gloves. The most popular men's colognes of the day were **British Sterling, Brut, English Leather,** and **HiKarate.** I tried them all, separately and in combination. Still, I could never rest easy. The fear was always there that someone at school would wrinkle their nose and say, "I smell hogs."

*I dreaded Thursdays*, but they kept coming with regularity.

The tide began to turn on one particular Thursday morning. My father rousted me out of bed informing me that Pa Dave, as usual, had some pigs to be hauled. I got dressed and prepared for the worst, having no idea that it was coming.

 As I drove up to Pa Dave's feed barn that morning the hallway doors were open and he was no where in sight. I backed the truck up to the barn entrance, turned off the engine, and climbed out to see where the pigs where. As I  started down the hallway, Pa Dave stepped out of the stable at the far end of the barn. He tried to sound enthusiastic as he said, "They're back here, son." He opened the stable door for me to take a look and as he did, with a note of apology in his voice, he said, "They are a little big this time." Then his voice brightened a bit and he said, "But there's just five of them!" I could hardly believe the sight that met my eyes.

Now, there are feeder pigs and then there are hogs. These were hogs. Not just any kind of hogs. They were "old" enough to be mamas and daddies. The first word that came to my mind was "rangy." These suckers had spent some time in the woods and were as hard as rocks. The last time I had seen hogs like these was in the movie, "Old Yeller." I knew why Pa Dave had not sold them at lighter weights. You can't sell what you can't catch.

I quickly sized up the situation. Three of the "pigs" were similar in size. I estimated them to weigh between 100 and 120 lbs. One was smaller. I figured he weighted 85 lbs. The biggest one  weighed 135 lbs. if he weighed an ounce. I took note that the males had been castrated. If they had not, I would have feared for my life. When I stepped inside the stable to catch the first one, they did not squeal like pigs. They barked at me like a dog. They let out a collective "woof, woof, woof" as they ricocheted off the  stable walls. Then they all backed into one corner of the stable to defend themselves.

I knew that I had to get them to run away from me so I jumped up and down and hollered "su-eey." They obliged. Around the stable they crashed. I spotted a trailing hind leg and grabbed on. With his right leg in my right hand and his tail in my left, I dragged the first one through the stable door and down the hallway to the truck. I have never heard such squealing in my life. A mature hog can make some powerful noise. My ears would ring for the remainder of the day.

When I reached the back of the truck, Pa Dave arrived just in time to grab our quarry by the ears and help me roll him up on the tailgate of the truck. I pointed our captive through the stock gate. When I turned him loose, he almost jumped over the front of the truck rack. One down, four to go.

I repeated the process to load the other two that were similar in size. My plan was to catch my breath a bit as I loaded the smallest one. That would give me a chance to gather my wits and my strength before I took on "ole Sasquatch."

The senior member of our quintet was not only big, he was smart. He had observed the fate of his mates, and he would not be taken easily.

As I entered the stable for the final assault, I knew that he held at least one advantage over me. I was tired and he was fresh. I decided to let him run a little. I let out a war hoop and around and around the stable he sprinted. When he stopped to catch his breath, I closed in. As I did, he tried to dart past me. I caught his tail in my left hand and I held on. That's when I observed that he was bigger than I had figured. I swung his backside around and pointed him toward the open stable door. My strategy was to let *him* drag *me* out of the stable instead of *me* attempting to drag *him*. He bolted for the opening. As he pulled me through the door, I reached and grabbed his right rear leg just below his hock. What a leg on a hog! His leg was as big around as the big end of a baseball bat! I swung him around and started "crawfishing" him down the hallway.

That's when I realized how strong he was. I was as determined to get him in that truck as he was to jump out of the barn. Down the hallway we wrestled. I would drag him ten feet, and he would take back five feet. I was digging my feet into the hallway dirt so deep that a couple of times I found myself halfway up under him. I would leverage myself almost parallel to the ground, then back up two steps and pull again. And the squealing! This hog had a set of lungs!

Finally, we arrived at the back of the truck. When Pa Dave reached for his ears, the danged hog had enough left in him to try and bite him, but Pa Dave finally managed to grab the hog's left ear and twist his snout away. With that, I summoned my last bit of energy, hoisted his backside into the air, threw my knee under his belly and with Pa Dave's help, rolled him up the tailgate and into the truck.

I staggered back against the wall of the hallway and slid down into a squat with my arms crisscrossing my knees. I was so spent that I felt nauseous. As I began to gather myself, Pa Dave strolled over and asked, "Son, what do I owe you?"

I was too exhausted to think or care at the moment. So, I sighed, "Whatever you think is fair, Pa."

I had been set-up perfectly. He cheerfully replied, "Well, they tell me that the going rate is a quarter a head."

"*A quarter a head, a quarter a head,*" I could hear those words bouncing around in my tired brain like an echo in some distant canyon.

"*A quarter a head,*" I was trying to make sense of what he was saying.

What he had said was **partially** true. A quarter a head **was** the going rate if one was hauling **200** pigs over a distance of **50** miles in a double deck truck. That would have amounted to a $50.00 haul bill. I was being offered **one dollar and twenty-five cents** for manhandling five "souped-up" **wildcats** disguised as feeder pigs, not to mention hauling them to market.

I finally managed to say, "Just pay daddy the next time you see him." I really hadn't expected to be paid anyway.

I gave myself time to recover from what the old folks called "the weak trembles" and kicked off my boots. Then I pealed off my sweat-soaked coveralls, doused my body with the cologne of the day, HiKarate, and headed out for school by way of the feeder pig barn. I had learned a lesson  that would not soon be forgotten.

Two or three weeks later, I was informed by my father on a Wednesday night that Pa Dave had pigs to be hauled. I arrived at his farm bright and early on the next morning.

I stopped at the gate that led into the barn lot on that bright spring morning, hopped out of the truck, and threw the gate open, I pulled the truck through and closed the gate behind me. As I drove down to the feed barn, I noticed that one of the hallway doors was open and I could see the big livestock loading chute rolled in place. I wheeled the truck shapely to the right and backed up leaving the truck bed flush with the top of the loading chute. I stepped down out of the truck and headed into the barn.

That is when I heard Pa Dave bark this command, "Here, hold this door." With that, he threw open the stable door nearest to the bottom end of the loading chute. It caught neatly on the outside post of the chute creating a perfect pathway out of the stable, up the loading chute, and onto the truck. He then waded out into what sounded like a stable *filled* with **little pigs**, much like a man wading out into knee deep water. He cracked his horse whip a couple of times and let out a squall. As he did, a wave of feeder pigs came squealing and thrashing out of the stable. They were up the loading chute and onto the truck in less than 20 seconds. I had not lifted a finger!

I quickly followed them up and closed the truck gate. As I turned to climb back down the chute I heard Pa Dave in a rather triumphant voice call out, "Son, what do I owe you?"

With a note of admiration in my voice I asked, "Pa, how *many* pigs do you have here?"

"*Twenty-seven*," he beamed.

"Well," I said, "the last time you said the going rate was a quarter a head. That comes to *six dollars and seventy-five cents*."

I wish you could have been there to see the look on his face. He was **speechless**.

I waited.

It took a moment or two for him to regain his composure. Then all he could manage to say was, "Uh, uh, I'll just pay your daddy next time I see him." He didn't know that this little deal was not quite done.

When I arrived at the feeder pig market that morning, I gave the gentleman who wrote up the dock tickets these instructions, "Take **six dollars and seventy-five cents** out of Mr. McCall's check for hauling 'per Jack McCall'." I was very familiar with the process. After unloading the pigs, I drove the truck around the livestock barn to the business office. I walked into the office and requested that the bookkeeper issue me a check in the amount of six dollars and seventy-five cents, to be taken out of D. T. McCall's check for hauling. I knew that it would appear among the deductions on his check voucher. The bookkeeper cut my check on the spot. I stopped and cashed it on my way to school.

The next time that I heard from Pa Dave was, I guess you might say, **indirectly**. It was, after a few weeks had passed by, on a Thursday morning. My grandmother had called our house to check in on the day's activities. Somewhere in the conversation, my mother inquired, "What is Pa doing today?"

My grandmother replied, "I believe I saw his truck down at the barn a while ago. He must be hauling pigs."

He would never ask me to haul his pigs again. I guess the **"going rate"** was more than he was willing to pay.

My grandfather always seemed to be hard on his grandchildren, especially the ones with whom he interacted on a regular basis. I grew to understand that his approach to life was heavily influenced by the Great Depression. He had seen **hard times**. He often spoke of how, as a boy, he had worked for a **dime a day**.

Whenever his methods of dealing with us were questioned by my mother or grandmother, he would mockingly say, "I'm **learning** 'em." I suppose he was.

Things changed between him and me after the "**six dollar and seventy-five cent**" deal. Prior to that day, whenever my grandfather would ask my mother about me, he'd usually say, "How's Jack?" She noted that his voice would have a mocking smirk about it. After that day, his voice rang with admiration when he inquired about me. I must have won his respect the day I matched wits with him.

I've often thought about that day. Somehow I am not willing to give him credit for having the teaching genius of thinking, "I'll continue to take advantage of Jack until he stands up for himself." With that lesson and many others, I have come to understand that a **virtue** taken to an extreme can become a **vise**. I have always admired **peacemakers**. I am inclined to be one myself, by nature and by choice. If you are one, or know one, you are familiar with some of their qualities—accommodating, easygoing, low key. But if all those qualities that make up a peacemaker are not tempered with reason, one can find himself in trouble fast. There are people who will take you away! They will take advantage of you, run over you, dare I say, **use** you! Maybe that is why the greatest Teacher of all, when instructing His followers to be **harmless**, warned them first to be **wise**.

On the other hand, I have always admired those rugged individuals who are the hard charging, no nonsense, can do, all business types. But when taken to the extreme, there is so much that they seem to miss.

It comes down to reason and passion and how to **balance** them. It is one of life's most daunting challenges.

# *Chapter 9*

# High School Basketball

When I attended elementary school I played basketball. In those days there were two divisions of players on the boy's team, the big boys and the little boys. If you were 5 feet, 6 inches or under, you played for the little boys or junior boys.

Consistent with the times, there were multiple elementary schools throughout Smith County. The names were Difficult, Pleasant Shade, Forks of the River, Defeated, Union Heights, Cox Davis, New Middleton, Carthage, and Gordonsville.

Each year, at tournament time, all the teams gathered for the county championship. Of course, all players were measured to determine that all the junior boys met the height requirement. I remember, as an 8th grader, the day I walked into the room to be measured. The officials took one look at me at the door and said,  "he's okay." That's how easily I qualified. Because of my lack of size, I knew that it was pointless for me to tryout for the high school team when fall rolled around the following year. By my freshman year I had grown to 5 feet, 7 inches and weighed all of 115 lbs.

When I began my junior year in high school some of my friends had convinced me that I was good enough to play for the varsity team. So, with high hopes that year, I went out for the team. It is important to note that in the two years that had passed, I had grown another inch and added ten pounds to my slight frame. I now stood 5 feet, 8 inches tall and weighed 125 pounds.

To my absolute delight, I made the varsity basketball team at Smith County High School in 1968. The truth of the matter is that I was the thirteenth player on a thirteen-player team. I was, in the truest sense, a bench warmer. In those days basketball was played in a big, cold, open gym which was rather drafty at times. The bench was made up of metal chairs which became rather cold if unoccupied.

If a player came out of the game all hot and sweaty, you certainly didn't want him sitting on a cold seat. Might make him sick. So you had these bench warmers that kept the bench warm for other players.

It might also be noted that the only time I went into the game was when we were 35 points ahead or 35 points behind. The game was no longer in doubt when the coach sent me in. When I did get in the game my average playing time was something like 47 seconds.

One night I came home all excited and my mother said, "What is wrong with you?" I said, "I got to play tonight!" She said, "Well, you seem more excited than usual. What happened?" I said, "They threw me the ball." She said, "What did you do with it?" I said, "I lost it out of bounds."

On a few occasions the coach got really risqué and sent in five "B" team players at the same time. Talk about pandemonium! *If you got it, you shot it!* It was kind of dangerous to be out there. I mean, some of those guys got excited if they hit the backboard with the ball. In a word, my experience playing basketball as a junior in high school was "uneventful."

When my senior year began I changed my goal. Art Linkletter once said, "Set your goals, but don't set them in concrete." A mid-course correction was in order. I decided to raise the bar. I set my sights on becoming one of the starting five.

I approached the season with a renewed enthusiasm. But, as the season loomed closer and closer, I became aware of two realities. The first was that two of my friends were becoming very well established at the starting guard positions. Secondly, there were a couple of other "B" team players that seemed to be playing as much as I was. Little did I realize the seriousness of the situation. My fate was to be learned on a Friday afternoon.

Oh, the anticipation of youth! I had waited all week for 5th period on Friday. That was the time when the basketball roster would be posted on the bulletin board in the dressing room. In my mind's eye I can still picture my trip over to the gym that afternoon. As I left the wing of the high  school, I made my way across the parking lot through the double doors of the gym, took a left through two more double doors, and headed down the steps to the gym floor. I took a U-turn at the bottom of the steps, walked through the door which led to the dressing rooms, down two steps, took another left, and headed for the bulletin board at the end of the hall. When I arrived at the bulletin board, I turned to my left and scanned the posting of uniform numbers. **My heart almost stopped.** Not only had I not gotten my old number 21, *my name was not on the list.* I had not even made the team.

It's a great thing to live in a free society where you have options. After pulling myself back together, I decided that I had three. Option number 1: Go find the coach as soon as possible and tell him just exactly what I thought of him in no uncertain terms. When I got through with him a fly wouldn't light on him. (That's called making an emotionally charged decision.) Option number 2: Take my Converse tennis shoes (They've made a "come back.") and my gym shorts and join the ranks of the defeated, never to be heard from again. (It's called quitting.) Option number 3: Go back and keep trying. Of my three options, the hardest of all to face was option number 3.

The pool of players from which our coach had to choose was small at best. After choosing what he considered to be the best 13 players, what remained was not a pretty sight. For me to be left out there with them was almost more than I could bear. Some of those guys had to leave their gum in the dressing room because they couldn't negotiate the ball with their hands when gum was in their mouths at the same time.

What's more, the only time we would get to

scrimmage was after practice was over and the bus bell had rung. It was, at best, a disheartening situation.

I reviewed my options carefully. My parents had always emphasized the importance of a good reputation. And, I knew that if I pooled my collective ignorance and told the coach exactly what I thought of him that every time he saw me for the rest of my life, that's what he would have remembered about me. That eliminated Option number 1. And I could not bring myself to quit. That eliminated Option number 2. So, I arranged an interview with the coach. He agreed to see me on the following day, even said that he would be glad to see me. I made the trip down to see him that afternoon, walked into his office, and sat down across from him. He looked like a grizzly bear sitting behind his desk looking back at me. It was my moment of truth.

I pulled up all 5 feet, 8 inches of my 125 lb. frame, looked him square in the eye, and said, "Coach, I think you have made a mistake. I think I'm a better player than the player who got 'my' uniform. Then, I attempted to leverage my position by saying, "and there are some more players on this team that feel the same way I do." Lucky for me he did not ask for names!

He simply answered me by saying, "You may feel that way, but I am the coach."

Undeterred, I said, "I understand that and I respect your position." Then I tried a different approach. I said, "Coach, I am going to make a deal with you. If you will give me a chance for the next two weeks, I am going to show you what a mistake you have made. I am going to out play, out do, out hustle, out quick, out everything, not only this player that got "my suit," but 3 or 4 more players on this team."

To my complete surprise, he smiled and said, "Fair enough! We'll see what happens!"

At the end of two weeks he knew that he had made a mistake. I had delivered on my promise. The ball was in his court. Then something happened that neither of us had expected. The reserve string center quit because he wasn't getting to start off. I went in there just wanting a suit, and I ended up the reserve string center! Well, not really.

Now, if you will recall some statistical data that I mentioned earlier in this chapter, I was 5 feet, 8 inches tall and weighed 125 lbs. The reserve string center was 6 feet tall and weighed 175 lbs. And, his suit fit him! I remember my waist size was a tight-fitting 28; his was 34. I always marveled at the size of my chest, how small it was at 32 inches. His jersey was a 44. That night I took that uniform home to my mother and said, "Mother, take this and see what you can do." With the help of the Lord and a good sewing machine, she cut that thing down to where it was a reasonable fit. Of course, she had to take six inches out of the waist. That means she put gathers in **all the way around**. I was the first player in the history of organized sports to wear **pleated** basketball trunks. By the time she tightened the waist all the way down, the legs stuck out on the sides like a ballerina skirt. She had to put stitches down the side of the legs just to hold them in. Then she rolled the straps on the jersey and stitched them down. More rolls, more stitches! By the time she was finished, it looked like I had military uniform bars on the tops of my shoulders. She had to do that just to keep me from tucking the number 54 on the back down in my pants!

I'm sure that I was a sight to behold but what I looked like was not important. What counted most was how I *felt*. I remember in vivid detail the exhilaration that I felt the first night that I rejoined the team in warm-up drills. I was **back**! The stage was set!

Our basketball season, however, proved to be disappointing to the players and our coach. We won a few games at the beginning and then settled into losing 12 or 13 games in a row. It became a pattern that played itself out game after  game. After struggling through the first half, we would find ourselves 12 to 15 points behind by intermission and then suffer out the second half. The coach had tried everything to break the spell.  Nothing seemed to work. The last home game of the season came, almost as a welcome relief.

We were playing the Sparta Warriors on a Friday night. They had shellacked us up in White County earlier in the year.

That night the first half played out like all the others. At half time we were trailing by 15 points. The dye was cast. Three minutes into the second half, we were still behind by 13 points when the coach looked down the bench and called my name.

I thought he had left something in the dressing room at half time and wanted me to go get it! I slipped down the bench and knelt beside him. He said, "Jack, you are a senior. This is the last time you will ever play in this gym. Why don't you go in there and see what you can do?"

I could hardly believe it! If the Sparta coach had known who was going in the ball game at that time, he should have said to his team, "Boys, let's go get on the bus and get out of here while we can."

I remember how the sole on my right foot  tingled when I stepped across the baseline and entered the playing floor. It was electrifying! I raced on the floor to play basketball so far above my head that it was almost beyond imagination.

Something magical was happening. I was inspired, and whatever it was that I had, the team caught it too! Our defense was so stifling that one time I looked in the eyes of the guy I  was guarding on a 2/3 zone defense and he looked so frustrated I felt sorry for him. We made all the right passes, took all the right shots, hustled every play. The hometown crowd, sensing a comeback, came alive. In what seemed like a dream to me, we went from a 15-point deficit to a 5-point lead. With three minutes left on the clock, the coach took me out of the game. I guess he was afraid that I might blow the ending. It might have been good coaching.

We won the game by 3 points. It was one of the great moments of my life! Because that night, in that gym, in a tiny, rural high school in Middle

Tennessee, I learned what it is like to be a *champio*n. I have been to the mountain top. I *know* the feeling inside.

In 1978, the University of Kentucky won the NCAA Men's Basketball Championship in St. Louis, Missouri. I was sitting on the living room floor of my parents home watching that game on television. At the end of the game, the Kentucky players were absolutely delirious.NCAA Champions! Rick Roby, their center, was all of 7 feet tall, and it appeared that he was jumping six feet off the floor. I have never seen a group of boys more jubilant. As I sat there watching the celebration, I wondered if those boys felt as good as I did the night that I became a *champion*. Before I stopped wondering, I wished that they felt nearly as good as I did the night we beat Sparta!

They do not remember me for my basketball prowess back at Smith County High School. I have not been back for a **Jack McCall Day**. My fading picture does not grace the halls of my alma mater nor can it be found in a trophy case. If all my playing time were added together, it would not amount to a complete game—32  minutes. I scored <u>5</u> points in my two-year career. They don't remember me back at my hometown high school, but I will *never* forget the lesson that I learned there. Sometimes our most memorable experiences and greatest life lessons take place in the most obscure settings.

And so it was for me. In the darkest moments of my high school basketball experience, when I discovered that I had not made the team, and

I struggled to make sense of the situation, I questioned everything that I had been taught.

One of the basic life principles taught in the home where I grew up was this: *If you act right, talk right, live right and do right, everything will work out right.*

It was a few years later, in Economics 101 at the University of Tennessee that I was first introduced to and understood the concept of the *short run and the long run*. Sometimes we must endure disappointment, disenchantment, failure, and even heartbreak in the "short run" as a proving ground for what lies in store for us in the "long run."

# Chapter 10
# School Bus Driver

After my older brother left home for college in the late 1960s, my father started driving a school bus.  His bus route allowed my father to be back on the farm by 8:30 a.m. each morning. Upon leaving his farm work at 2:00 p.m. for what he called the "afternoon run," he could return to complete his evening chores before dark. Because of the irregular labor demands of a working farm, the bus driving job fit into his schedule well. The extra cash flow was also welcome.

 I never really gave much thought to the fact that my father had chosen to supplement his farm income by driving a school bus. During my high school days it did create a minor inconvenience for me. It was necessary for **someone** to drop off a vehicle at the school bus garage in town each morning for my father's return trip home. Then, that vehicle had to be picked up and driven back home in the afternoon by **someone**. That **someone** usually ended up being me. On most mornings my father would arrive early enough to drop me off at school. In the afternoons I either **hitched** a ride to the bus garage or I was in for a long walk. All in all, it became part of a routine that worked. That big yellow bus became a familiar part of the landscape on our farm. Like I said, I never gave it much thought. That is, until I left home for college.

Going *away* to college does many things for a person. For one, it forces us to see our world through different eyes. When I say our world, I mean the safe familiar world in which we grew up. We begin to see our world through the eyes of other people. I was not too far into my college career when I began to go home with friends for the weekend and bring friends home with me. In my mind that school bus suddenly became an issue.

If it happened once, it happened a dozen times. Whenever I brought a new friend, male or female, home with me for the weekend, here's how the conversation played out. As we crossed the last hill that overlooked the little valley were the road turned toward our farm, I would point to the right and say, "that's our farm." And *every* time, my friend would ask, "what's that school bus doing there?" I would answer under muffled breath, "my father drives a school bus." My friend would answer, "Oh." It didn't seem like a big deal to them. But it bothered me. For whatever reason, I felt a sense of shame that my father was supplementing his farm income by driving a school bus. The "old folks" would have said that "I had gotten above my raisin" or that I had become "too big for my britches." There I was, Mr. College Hot Shot, on the one hand having great respect for my father, and on the other hand feeling ashamed of what he was doing. It made me feel a strong sense of dislike for myself. It also showed that I still had a lot to learn.

In the fall of 1978, I was re-introduced to my high school sweetheart, Kathy Oakley. I had only seen her twice in the preceding 10 years. We immediately renewed our courtship and exchanged wedding vows on her birthday the following year. Two became one on September 1, 1979, and two became three on May 31, 1980. We named him, James Brim McCall after Kathy's father and my maternal grandfather. We called him J. Brim.

I cannot describe how I felt the first time that I held him in my arms. It ranks among the best moments in my life, and I have been blessed with more than my share. But I must confess, as I thought about our son during those first hours of his life, I began to look ahead. And as I did, I dreaded the day that that **BIG YELLOW MONSTER** (school bus) would come to a stop in front of my house, open its folding door mouth, and swallow up my boy and take him away. But a few years later it did. That's when my opinion of school bus drivers changed dramatically.

We had some good ones over the years. I think Mr. Burnley was our favorite. He was a tall, good looking man with a friendly voice and a broad smile that flashed gold in his teeth. One day, J. Brim, a kindergartener, was supposed to get off the bus at his grandmother Oakley's house. Seems that he forgot. When Mr. Burnley reached the end of his route, our boy was still on the bus. That day Kathy got a phone call. The conversation started something like this, "K-a-t-h ñy, I believe I got sumpun down here at my house belongs to you." It was Mr. Burnley. He was as safe with Mr. Burnley as he would have been with me.

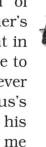

Since those days I have thought often of school bus drivers. I can still recall my father's routine of cranking his bus engine at daylight in the winter to give the engine and the bus time to warm up. In all the years that he drove, he never had an accident. I have thought of a school bus's precious cargo, each child as precious to his parents as our boys are to us. It has taught me along with other experiences that *everyone* and *the job they do* is important.

That lesson was re-affirmed for me a few years back when my father died. During the time of visitation before his funeral, the people came. Hundreds and hundreds came. I wondered, *who are all these people?* Most were too young to be friends of my parents or friends of their children. As my brothers, my sister, and I began to greet the long line of those who had come to show their respect, it all became clear. A typical conversation went something like this, "You probably don't know me. Mr. Frank was my school bus driver. I loved him so much."

School bus drivers, I had the high privilege of knowing and loving one of the best among them. And somewhere along the way, I picked up on one of life's great lessons—the fact that *everyone* fills an important role and that we *all* need each other—that it takes *each* of us making his or her contribution if we are to make a better world.

## Chapter 11

# Uncle Dave Manning

It is strange how, and sometimes why, we keep some customs alive. I understand that before the advent of funeral homes, the dead were kept at home until buried. Out of that reality was born a ritual that we in the South called "staying up with the dead" or "staying up with the body." In the early days of this country, before there were screened doors and screened windows, it was necessary to keep a "watch" over the deceased simply to keep the dogs and cats from "bothering" the body. As society became more sophisticated and homes were built to be varmint proof, the custom continued purely out of respect for the deceased. Even after bodies  were no longer kept at home, friends, neighbors and family would gather and keep all night vigils at the local funeral home until the day of the funeral service. Many considered it one of the rites of final passage, but it is more than that. It was a time for reflecting, a time for showing one's final respects. There might be a crowd early in  the evening but the crowd would begin to thin out as the night progressed. By the wee hours of the morning, the number gathered would be small.

Sitting up with the body can be a wonderful time for reminiscing—a time of recalling fond memories of the deceased. Each member of the vigil would take turns recalling their personal recollections of the one "gone on."

This brings us to the evening of September 21, 1981, at Sanderson's Funeral Home in Carthage, Tennessee. My great uncle, Dave Manning, had died and a few friends and neighbors were gathered for the first evening's watch.

I had a special fondness for "Uncle" Dave. His wife, who had predeceased him, was named Mattie. In life, they were inseparable. It seemed like you never referred to one without including the other. It was always "Uncle Dave and Aunt Mattie." As a boy, I always looked forward to our yearly invitation to visit them "along about the Fourth of July." Uncle Dave's fame as a  watermelon grower was widespread. Our annual visit always culminated in a trip to watermelon heaven. I would watch with childlike wonder as my father and Uncle Dave thumped prospective melons checking for ripeness. As they listened to the sound made by their thumps, each would nod or shake his head in unison with each other  as to whether the melon was ripe or not. Each boy (there were four of us) left the patch loaded with a melon that matched our load-bearing ability. Those were good days.

Uncle Dave, who was actually my great uncle, was the uncle that my father "took after" or "favored" most. Their physical build was almost identical. Both had the same sweet, unassuming smile that bordered on shyness.

But now Uncle Dave was dead, and a small number of men were gathered after midnight.

The evening was hushed, the conversation low and reverent.

Among the group was a neighbor named Sam A. Denton. He and his wife were like Uncle Dave and Aunt Mattie, inseparable. We always called them "Mr. Sam A." and "Miss Johnnie Mae." Everyone in the small group had recalled their best memory of Uncle Dave. Now, it was Mr. Sam A.'s turn.

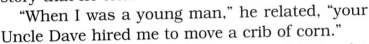

Sam A. Denton was a sensitive man—prone to show his emotions if the subject ran deep. Really great men, I think, are comfortable with their emotions. Mr. Sam A. could "tear up" easily. His eyes were "watering" as he began. This is the story that he told.

"When I was a young man," he related, "your Uncle Dave hired me to move a crib of corn."

Now I must inform the reader that there's a lot more to this than one might suspect. A crib, for the purpose of definition, is a holding area with a raised wood floor used to store ear corn. The job entailed physically scooping the corn into a mule wagon, hauling it five or six miles and scooping it into another crib in a different location. Hence, "moving the crib of corn."

Mr. Sam continued, "Your Uncle Dave didn't know how many wagon loads were involved but we agreed on the price of a dollar a load."

"On Monday morning I went to work. If I worked hard, I could turn around two loads in a day. Of course, at the start and end of each day, the mules had to be caught, harnessed, or unharnessed and fed. By late Friday, the job was finished."

"On Saturday morning I went to his house to get my pay as we had agreed beforehand," mused Mr. Sam A.

"Your Uncle Dave came out of the house and met me on the front porch. He greeted me by saying, "Well Sam, how many loads did you have?" I said, "Mr. Dave, there were nine loads in all." He smiled as he retrieved his billfold from the bib of his overalls. Then he pulled a crisp, just like new, ten-dollar bill out of his billfold and said, "Well, Sam, you earned nine, but I am going to pay you for ten."

Mr. Sam A.'s chin was quivering and his eyes were running over with tears as he concluded his story by saying, "I will never forget his generosity. A dollar was a lot of money back then. And I could use that extra dollar."

Of all the stories told that night, his was most memorable. A simple act of generosity treasured for a lifetime.

# Chapter 12

# Pinto Beans, Cornbread and Sorghum Molasses

I've met more than a few unforgettable characters in my time. One of my favorites was Bob Dudney. Mr. Dudney was someone who always had a sparkle of mischief in his eyes and something **good** to say; and a story—**always** a story to tell. Of the ones he told me, the following is my all time favorite.

In the early part of his career, Bob Dudney worked in one of the divisions of the Department of Agriculture. ASCS, I believe. But, it could have been the Forestry Service. At any rate, within his job description, he was given the task of selling landowners on a new tree harvesting program that had been ushered in as a part of Roosevelt's *New Deal*.

He described the program to me as being a **godsend** to rural landowners, especially to those who owned tracts of timber that had not been harvested. The program entailed a process by which, with the help of government specialists, **mature** trees would be marked for harvest, a logging company contracted, and then, seedlings replanted. The completed process would result in the landowner being presented with a check for more money than many had ever seen. Everyone would come out a winner.

It all sounded well and good, but Mr. Dudney was to encounter two major problems. Number One: He was to sell the program in rural Jackson County in what was known as *moonshining country*. Number Two: He worked for the Federal government and was going into *moonshining country*. As he related the story to me, he smiled and admitted, "You know, some of those *government* people went into *moonshining country* and never came back." So, he had his work cut out for him. Indeed, one particular landowner provided my friend with a unique challenge.

Initially, he made contact with this landowner by way of the U.S. Mail. Letters were exchanged and after no small amount of encouragement, the man agreed to a personal visit from a representative of the government.

On the appointed day, Mr. Dudney drove his pick-up truck into one of the most remote parts of Jackson County. At the end of a lonely gravel road, he left his truck and walked another two miles on a mule path. A *general sense of uneasiness* came over him as he ventured further and further into the back country.

*Finally*, the homestead came into view. It was one of those clap board houses built into the side of a hill, one with an unusually high front porch and a severely slopping front yard.

Two friendly dogs barked and rushed off the hill and greeted him at the edge of the yard wagging their tails in an exaggerated fashion.

Hearing the commotion, the father led the

entire family out the door and they lined up on the front porch and peered down at their visitor. Mr. Dudney noticed how they all were dressed. The head of the house wore overalls and high-top, clodhopper work shoes. The boys sported one-piece ensembles: overalls and barefeet. The wife and daughters were dressed alike in cotton print dresses with matching bonnets, and the entire family wore suspicious looks.

With an uneasy smile, the father invited the stranger to join him, and their meeting convened on the front porch. Bob Dudney embarked on the sales challenge of his life.

The discussion proceeded awkwardly and had an **uncomfortable feel** about it. Every benefit of the tree harvesting program that Mr. Dudney presented was met with an objection. Some objections were reasonable, most were born of ignorance and suspicion. The morning dragged on. Minimal progress was made.

As lunch time approached, the mother appeared in the open front door more than once and each time she seemed more ill at ease not sure what to do about this stranger and lunch. Mr. Dudney was now trying a new strategy. He had decided to **wait them out**. Finally, seeming a bit exasperated, the mother came out on the porch and asked if he would like to join them for "dinner." Mr. Dudney **allowed** that he would be pleased to join them for a meal. He was invited to come in the house, and as he stepped through the front door, this is the scene that he described.

In the center of the room sat a large, rough hewn, kitchen table. Long benches provided seating down each side of the table. Matching armed, straight-back chairs were placed at each end.

In the center of the table, sat a large kettle of pinto beans, still gurgling from the heat of the fire. Next to the kettle sat a big, black skillet of corn bread, along side it was a half gallon bucket of sorghum molasses. Glasses of clear, cold spring water were placed beside each plate. The mother was pouring scalding hot coffee into cups for the adults as each took his place around the table.

Everyone took a seat—but, then no one moved. It was one of those awkward moments when no one seemed to know what to do. There were some confused glances and questioning looks. Mr. Dudney suddenly realized that this family had **never** had a stranger at their table. They did not know what to do next.

Sometimes desperate situations call for desperate measures. Mr. Dudney noticed the steam slowly rising from his coffee cup and suddenly he had an idea. He grabbed the steaming cup and carefully tipped it, allowing half of its contents to run into his saucer. Leaning forward, he **blew** his breath across the coffee in the saucer. The steam billowed. He **blew** some more. Then he placed his lips on the edge of the saucer and gave the coffee an exaggerated "*s-l-u-r-r-p.*"

When he had finished, the mother moaned a deep sight of relief and immediately, one of the children called out, "pass the beans." Suddenly, the room came to life! "Dinner" was underway! Conversation was now engaging and upbeat and "covered every subject under the sun." Never had pinto beans and cornbread tasted so good! After second and third helpings, *everyone* was satisfied. It was time to move back to the front porch and relax.

Negotiations began as a carryover of the conversation at the kitchen table. After a very few minutes, the landowner asked if there were papers to sign. Documents were produced. Signatures penned. The deal was done!

I've often thought of this story and the skills employed by my now deceased friend. He was, I think, what we would call a "country psychologist." There is something to be said for those who are comfortable enough with themselves and have the compassion to set others at ease.

The ability to **connect** with other human  beings is, sadly, becoming a dying art. Why do we insist on making that which is so profoundly simple, so difficult?

I think it was Confucius who said, "When you are in the presence of a person of higher social standing, leave him with a good opinion of *yourself.* When in the presence of a person of lower standing, leave him with a good opinion of *himself.*"

## Chapter 13

# My Toughest Customer Ever

How I ended up on his farm, I'm not really sure. My career in livestock marketing had taken me to Northern Middle Tennessee where I was manager of a new multimillion-dollar livestock market. There was a new cattle buyer in the area and it was me. Somehow, I got the word that a man by the name of Duncan, in Sumner County, had a string of cattle that he wanted to sell "directly off the farm." That is risky business for the buyer and the seller—especially the buyer. I would have to proceed with caution. I met him at his farm on a late summer's morning. Initial greetings were friendly enough. Then he spent the better part of an hour going to some effort to convince me just how tough a man he was. He let me know, in no uncertain terms, that he believed in an hour's work for an hour's pay, especially when he was doing the paying. Hippies were on  their way out in the late 1970s, but he took the opportunity to let me know how "sorry" the young people of our day had become. Then he told me how he had hired "one of them no goods" just a few weeks back, but he let the boy know right from the start what he expected. He described the unsuspecting target of his wrath as having "that long yeller" hair. Then he smiled a devilish smile and said, "I put him to hand stripping hardwood floors in an old house that I was remodeling." Then, he conceded with the same devilish smile mingled with amusement that the work was hard. "But, I didn't let up on him. I would stick my head in the room every few minutes or so and holler 'get to work in there.'" He related that by lunch time "that boy was too tired to eat. He just laid under a tree and moaned until we went back to work." Mr. Duncan smiled triumphantly and said, "Ole yeller hair didn't show up for work the next day. One day of me was all he could stand." It made sense to me. Don't think I would have come back either.

By the time our interview was over, I was convinced that this man ate nails for breakfast and put a gravel in his shoes each morning before he laced them up just to remind himself of how tough he really was.

His cattle situation was no less unique than the man. I could not believe what I found when we arrived to look them over. There, scattered before me, like a prairie filled with buffalo, stood the most varied array of cattle I had ever seen on one farm. He explained rather casually that he had not sold any cattle in four years. Consequently, from his fifty mamma cows he had 3-year-old "calves," some weighing in excess of 1,000 lbs., 2-year-old "yearlings" most weighing between 600-900 lbs., and calves weighing from 250-550 lbs. Some were fat, some were thin, some in medium flesh, all were black, and he wanted one price per pound for the heifers and one price for the steers. It was a formidable challenge for a livestock buyer twice my age and experience. I recognized immediately that I was well in over my head. I opted for back up by offering to bring my company's most experienced order buyer on the scene to sort through the maze. That was acceptable to him. A few days later, our buyer came, they agreed on a price, and a deal was struck, but the job was far from being over.

On the day the cattle were to be sorted and weighed, we arrived on Mr. Duncan's farm at first light, per his instructions. The day was breaking with a sogginess about it; the air was permeated with the kind of heat and staleness that speaks of rain. The main feed barn, being ill-situated on the side of a hill, made it impossible for a tractor-trailer to make an approach. Therefore, the day's plan included loading small groups of calves on a single axle "bob" truck and shuttling each load to the bottom of the hill to be loaded on an 18-wheeler. Built in the mule days, the barn was also ill-equipped for sorting cattle. The halls were wide, the stable doors narrow. This was complicated by the fact that years of accumulating manure made the stable floors about a foot higher than the hallways. The threat of rain forced a stepped up pace all day long. The cattle did not react well to strangers, and on top of it all, Mr. Duncan was being his cantankerous self.

I was given the impossible task of acting as door man nearest the man responsible for sorting the cattle. Time after time after time, I would look up to see five or six, wild eyed calves bearing down on me, ahead of some voice out of the darkened hallway wailing, "catch the one in the middle." If I should miss the right calf or catch the wrong calf, which I did repeatedly, Mr. Duncan would appear at my side jerking the stable door out of my hands as he growled," don't you do that again." The day was not unfolding as I had hoped; instead, it continued to come unraveled for me.

By mid-afternoon I was beat. Because of the ominous signs of rain I had chosen to wear black "over-shoes" that day, the kind with metal buckles that buckle all the way to the knee. Hauling those things around all day is a day's work in itself. So, when I say "I was beat," I mean it in every way, mentally, emotionally and physically. No one drew more relief from seeing the last load pull away from that old barn than I did. I cannot recall when I ever felt like being more of a failure. I suspected that I would never be on this man's farm again.

As I started down the hill to the waiting tractor-trailer, my feet felt like concrete blocks, but they were not any heavier than my heart. When I finally made it to the bottom of the hill, the rain that had been holding off all day finally arrived.

First, it appeared as big single raindrops, the cold, heavy kind that stings the skin. Then, the summer dust began to take on little craters, some the size of silver dollars, as the raindrops bore in. The dust was settled in a moment and a muddy paste began to form on top of the ground. Lightning flashed in the west and drew my attention back to the barn.

The barn looked like a tired old sentry poised against the backdrop of the darkened sky. Already the western horizon had begun clearing, leaving a luminous ribbon of orange light cutting behind the threatening dark clouds. For a moment, I stopped to take in the splendor of the contradiction that lay before me.

Then I saw him.

Mr. Duncan was struggling to move the massive cattle-loading chute back in place. I must digress for a moment to describe that with which he was struggling. Most farms of that day were equipped with a loading chute much like his. It was a simple contraption consisting primarily of two large iron wheels about 36 inches in diameter, joined by a four-foot axle. Along the ends of the axle, near the wheel, two large oak timbers were balanced in the center of each, creating a seesaw effect. The timbers supported a layer of boards, which created the floor. Gates on each side provided for the funnel effect. The high end of the chute would rest against the truck bed at floor level and allow cattle to "climb" up the shoot. They were simple, functional, strong and *heavy*. I would guess one to weigh about 1/2 a ton, and moving one was not a one-man job. If one tried to move it by rolling one wheel, it would mock you by taking you in a circle. You couldn't pull it, and you could not push it unless you lifted one end, and one's back muscles could not effectively be used to push and lift at the same time. The situation literally created a comedy of errors.

Mr. Duncan was in a bind and I knew it. Instantly the question exploded on my mind. Should I or shouldn't I?

As I stood, over a hundred yards away, at the foot of the hill, a thousand thoughts, pictures and feelings flashed in my mind's eye. Fatigue, frustration, a sense of failure, instant replays of mistakes I had made during the day, his scowl— there were a thousand reasons not to go to his rescue. Then strangely, my upbringing got the best of me. I knew what I had to do. Breaking into a full sprint, I headed up the hill.

As I covered the distance between us, the newly formed mud began to cake to the bottom of my boots creating a one-inch doughy lip around the edges of each boot. I covered most of the run with an extra five pounds of weight on each foot. As I arrived at the top of the hill I realized that the long run had caused me to sweat through both shirts. Suddenly, I was at his side, my lungs heaving from the exertion of the run.

I quickly threw my weight against the wheel opposite his and we easily rolled the chute alongside the barn. I noticed that the inside wheel had found a familiar depression which signaled its return "home." But the job was not completed until Mr. Duncan took a chain, which had a steel ring at the end, and dropped it over a metal hook fixed on the side of the barn.

Then, Mr. Duncan, the old blood and guts,

tough as nails farmer turned to face me, and I looked into the eyes of a man that I had never seen before.

Oh, it was Mr. Duncan for sure, but now, his eyes were soft and warm, and in a kind, low voice he said, "Thank you, boy. You are the only one in this whole outfit that's got their heart in this."

I dropped my eyes and softly replied, "Thank you, sir." I turned to race off that hill with those mud laiden boots that had miraculously been transformed into ballerina slippers. But even so, they were not as light as my heart.

I was never on Mr. Duncan's farm again. From that day forward he brought the cattle that he had for sale to my livestock market. He never came inside—too busy. He just left these instructions with the man who wrote the dock tickets, "Tell Jack to take care of me."

One never knows what payoffs lie at the end of the extra mile until you have reached its end.

## Chapter 14
# Motivational Speech

I am always up to making a motivational speech. As a matter of fact I love to make motivational speeches. But, to be perfectly honest with you, I missed the birth of one of our sons because of a motivational speech. I know you might be thinking—you dirty dog you. You were off somewhere making a speech while your wife was at the hospital having that baby. That is low down. Well, it wasn't quite that way.

When our first son was born, it was as you would expect a very momentous occasion. My wife, Kathy, was naturally a little apprehensive about the birth experience. Especially due to the fact that the day we married she weighed 103 lbs. and the day she delivered she weighed every ounce of 155 lbs. The doctors had told us she was going to have a big baby. In my family, all my brothers and sisters were big babies, so we were prepared for a difficult delivery. The night he was born we went to the doctor's office about 10:30 p.m. and he sent us back home to walk. We walked until about 11:30 p.m. and then arrived back at the hospital. The doctor informed us that it was about time.

We went into the labor room and were there from 11:30 p.m. until 1:30 a.m. at which time Kathy gave birth to an 8 lb., 15-1/4 oz. boy! "We" came away from that experience with a very healthy attitude about having babies. She said, "You know it wasn't that bad." Now, I am not saying that she didn't experience some pain, but delivering a baby of that size in two hours—well it wasn't bad at all. So, whenever the subject of having more children came up, she had no objections.

Sixteen months later, we were back at the hospital to have our second. We arrived at the hospital about 11:30 p.m. and Kathy checked into the labor room. Things progressed normally, very methodically, until about 1:30. At that point we were halfway home (5 centimeters) and everything was looking great. And, then 1:30 turned into 2:30, 2:30 to 3:30, 3:30 to 4:30, 5:30 to 6:30, 6:30 to 7:30 and no progress had been made. By this time the only thing that had really changed was that the birth pains were coming  more rapidly and were more severe. After being in labor for 8 hours, Kathy was about spent. I have never seen a woman that was more whooped in my life. There was not a dry thread on her. Her hair was soaking wet and matted and stuck to the side of her head. She has these beautiful sad, pale-blue eyes and they were as pale and sad as I had ever seen them. She is a natural blonde and her skin is fair with blonde freckles and you could see every freckle. At this point **all** the color had drained from her face.

In a moment of great despair, she looked at me and in this pitiful voice she whispered, "Jack, what am I going to do? I am **s-o-o-o** tired. I don't think I can make it." As I looked into her sad, blue eyes I realized that what this situation called for was a motivational speech! I looked deeply into those sad, blue eyes and with all the enthusiasm I could muster, I said, "Honey, if you can hang on for just a few more minutes it will all be over!"

Now, that's motivation! The results were instantaneous. All that color that had drained from her face—it came back! Suddenly, the look of despair and hopelessness left her face as she sat up in that bed and yelled at me through clenched teeth, **"What do you know about it? You don't know that! And, you don't know how bad I'm hurting! I could be here all day!"** In that same moment, her eyes flared wide open and she screeched, **"I want to push; I want to push!"**

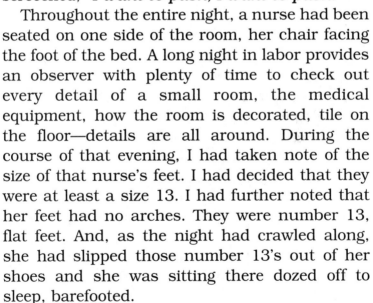

Throughout the entire night, a nurse had been seated on one side of the room, her chair facing the foot of the bed. A long night in labor provides an observer with plenty of time to check out every detail of a small room, the medical equipment, how the room is decorated, tile on the floor—details are all around. During the course of that evening, I had taken note of the size of that nurse's feet. I had decided that they were at least a size 13. I had further noted that her feet had no arches. They were number 13, flat feet. And, as the night had crawled along, she had slipped those number 13's out of her shoes and she was sitting there dozed off to sleep, barefooted.

When my wife cried out, "I want to push. I want to push," that nurse's eyes popped wide open. She raised her feet about three feet in the air and then slapped them down on the floor. When her big feet hit the floor, it made a sound much like a beaver slapping his tail against the smooth surface of a lake. I mean it clapped like a clap of thunder and she squalled out, "Oh, my gosh, honey, don't push, don't push! Get the doctor! Get the doctor!"

She bolted through the door and returned with the doctor in no more than ten seconds. The room exploded into activity as nurses came from every direction. They grabbed up Kathy, loaded her onto a gurney, rushed her into the delivery room, and I saw the door swing shut in my face. In the maddening rush they completely forgot about *me*!

Within what must have been only one minute, I heard from behind the doors of the delivery room the birth of our second son. But, I wasn't in there. I had missed this momentous event because of that motivational speech!

Two weeks later, when my wife was speaking to me again, out of nowhere, she looked at me and said, "How did you know?"

I really played it cool. I said, "Know what?"

She said, "How did you know I was going to have that baby in the next two minutes?"

I must confess, I did not tell her because I did not want to take anything away from the blessedness of the occasion. But, I had grown up on a farm. And, on that farm, I had spent hundreds of hours in a furrowing house, you know—the shed where baby pigs are born. Over the years, I had witnessed the birth of hundreds, no, thousands, of baby pigs. When you spend that much time with that many females delivering that many pigs, you develop a sixth sense as it relates to the female psyche. So I knew! But, I just couldn't tell her exactly *how* I knew.

Over the years I have gained an incredible respect for the spoken word. I believe that the right words, spoken at the right time, can have an incalculable impact! Just ask Kathy.

# Chapter 15

# Choo Choo

It is strange how children and their experiences are so different. My older brother Tom was a committed "thumb sucker." Everything was tried to get him to stop. My mother, in collaboration with one of my aunts, tried soaking his thumb in hot sauce before bed one night. It didn't work. During the night he woke up and washed his thumb and went right back at it.

I didn't suck my thumb. As a matter of fact, I gave up the baby bottle early as a toddler because I dropped mine on the hearth. The glass bottle broke and I got a cut. That ended it for me. My mother has said that I could eat the "middle" out of half a dozen biscuits soaked in red-eye gravy by the time I could hold my head up. My brother, John, drug around a baby bottle of chocolate milk until he was old enough to start to school.

We didn't have pacifiers in my house when I was growing up. But, by the time our first son was born, pacifiers had become extremely popular. Pacifiers have evolved, you know. Twenty years ago it was a very simple thing— disk, bulb, and handle. They are very sophisticated today. The disk has a grove in the top so it won't touch the child's nose. The bulb (or nipple) is flat on the bottom. And now, they come with a shoestring and clothespin that allows you to attach it to the little one's shirt so he won't **drop** it. Shoot, when our son dropped his on the floor or ground, we just picked it up, licked it off and stuck it back in his mouth. A little dirt is good for anybody.

Even the name "pacifier" evolved in our house. Someone called it a "fooler," someone else a "foo foo." Our son, J. Brim, settled on the word, "Choo Choo." He l-o-v-e-d his Choo Choo! No  matter how upset he became or how badly things seemed to be going for him, if he could get his hands on Choo Choo and pop it in his mouth, all would be right with the world! If Choo Choo became misplaced, we were in serious trouble. There was no substitute.

On one memorable evening Choo Choo came up missing. At first we didn't  panic, but as the evening went on things grew more desperate. We literally turned our house upside down in search of his lost treasure. Finally, around midnight, in desperation we called my father-in-law, a pharmacist, and begged him to open the drug store. We drove our son to town and he waited in the car as I ran inside the store. I reached inside the plastic bucket and grabbed the first one that I touched. It was yellow. I ran out to the car and handed it to our son who was waiting expectantly. He took one look at the "yellow" Choo Choo and burst into tears! Stupid dad, **everyone** should know that Choo Choo is **BLUE**! Back inside I ran. When I returned with the blue one, his face broke into a smile that would warm a father's heart. All was right with the world again.

Not only did our son love his Choo Choo, but he also mastered its use. I declare, a race car engine could not turn a piston faster than he could gum his Choo Choo. I calculated that he could work that thing at a rate of about one hundred and seventy-five strokes a minute! And, when he grinned, it didn't slow down! He made it seem as though it were floating in his mouth.

His baby brother, Jonathan, had been at home with us for about two months when J. Brim turned an ordinary evening into a lifetime memory for me.

On this particular night, I had been designated as the one to get big brother off to sleep. His mother was quietly rocking his little brother. As I gathered J. Brim up, I allowed him to perch on my left arm. When we started down the hall to the bedroom I noticed that we were dressed alike. He was wearing a diaper and no shirt. I was wearing boxers and no shirt. We were skin to skin. And Choo Choo was getting the workout of its life in my left ear. He had that thing singing!

As we entered the half darkened bedroom, I laid him on the bed and then awkwardly crawled over him to get to the middle of the bed. I remember the street light streaming in through the Venetian blinds. The room was dark, but not completely.

I laid down on my stomach and turned my head facing away from him. I had learned as a young father to disestablish eye contact to get little ones to sleep. I waited a moment. Then I peaked to see what he was doing.

He was mimicking me. He, too, was lying on his stomach with his head turned away from me and he was smiling through his Choo Choo. He seemed so pleased with himself. There we were, father and son, lying on our stomachs, looking in opposite directions. I have no idea what he was thinking. I was wondering how long it would take for him to drift off to sleep.

At that moment, I **heard** him pluck his pacifier out of his mouth. I wondered what he was up to. I decided to pretend that I was asleep. I almost missed it. But, I **heard** it and I *felt* it as he **kissed** me softly on my left shoulder. He popped Choo Choo back in his mouth. Then, he laid his fat little hand on the spot that he had just kissed and he patted me tenderly *three* times. I counted. Never had a hand so small delivered so much affection.

I lay there and tried not to move. I squeezed my sides with my arms trying not to laugh and trying not to cry, caught somewhere between the two. My eyes began to run over with tears and my heart became as light as a feather. And, in the quiet night, I loved that little boy who was now fast asleep. And, I thought within myself that I would have lived a lifetime to experience these tender moments, when a little boy, without saying a word, delivered a message to his father that went something like this, "Dad, for whatever you have invested in me so far, here's a return on your investment, '*I love you, too.*'"

Kahlil Gibran spoke of those who were afraid of taking the risks of love as ones who would pass "into a seasonless world where you shall laugh, but not with all your laughter, and weep, but not all of your tears."

Life is continuously calling us to participate more fully, more deeply, and more humanly. May you have the courage to love in spite of all the risks.

# Chapter 16
# Potty Training 101

I am convinced that raising a family is a trial by fire. I mean, where can you learn all that you need to know to take a child from birth to some reasonable state of independence? I didn't hear about any courses on the subject in either high school or college. There are those who say that the very fate of civilization rests on the maintaining of a healthy family unit. I believe that's true. Where else can you absorb so much of the basic stuff that is fundamental to nurturing a miniature human being. I know. I know. There are books on the subject. Dr. Spock wrote one that everyone was quoting back in the 50s and 60s. Seems he was against spanking as a teaching technique. I understand that he dismissed temper tantrums as a form of self expression. When we were growing up, my mother allowed each of her five children two temper tantrums, *the first one and the last one.*

The first time one of us fell out in the floor kicking and screaming, my mother displayed her own unique form of self expression. We responded by learning self *control.*

I consider myself fortunate to be the second of five. It gave me the benefit of observing the bringing up of two younger brothers and a baby sister. So, I did learn something about *little* people, much of which one cannot learn from a book. Some things have to be learned by experience. For instance, my mother taught me to cup my hand over a little boy's *pistola* when changing his diaper. She instructed me that his *safety* (as in a firing arm) was never *on*.

When our first son was born, I knew to take the necessary safety precautions when taking off his diaper. I would pull the front of his diaper down and quickly place my cupped hand, palm down between him and me. The first time my wife observed my doing so, she, with a wrinkled nose, asked, "What are you doing?" I said, "I would rather be safe than saturated." She said, "He won't do *that*." I smiled.

A few days later we found ourselves at the changing table participating in a joint diaper changing. She was primary changer. I was playing the role of assistant to the changer. She removed the pins and pulled down the front of the diaper. When junior's plumbing felt the cool air of the room, he fired a perfect five foot pee rainbow across the wall. It arched just above the quilted cloud wall treatment.

Kathy's eyes almost popped out of her head as her astonished look turned into our collective laughter.

"The next time you could get it in the eye," I teased. There are some things that must be learned by experience. That brings us to the issue of potty training.

I can't say that I remember much about how my younger brothers were trained in the art of going to the bathroom. Little country boys grow up watching the adult men in their lives step behind trees and around the corners of buildings when mother nature calls. The transition from wearing cloth diapers to not wetting your britches just seemed like the natural thing to do. Indoor plumbing is simply another modern evil that has messed with our minds. Little wonder that the outhouse was called a *privy*.

Needless to say, Kathy and I were ill prepared when we came face to face with the challenges of potty training. Our first son, J. Brim, was blessed (or cursed) with a mega colon. He **hated** going to **big bathroom** (#2) for obvious reasons. That naturally meant that he didn't care for going to **little bathroom** (#1) either.

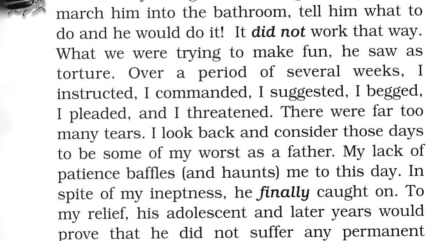

I honestly thought that on a given day I could march him into the bathroom, tell him what to do and he would do it! It **did not** work that way. What we were trying to make fun, he saw as torture. Over a period of several weeks, I instructed, I commanded, I suggested, I begged, I pleaded, and I threatened. There were far too many tears. I look back and consider those days to be some of my worst as a father. My lack of patience baffles (and haunts) me to this day. In spite of my ineptness, he *finally* caught on. To my relief, his adolescent and later years would prove that he did not suffer any permanent mental or emotional scares during his potty training days. I did not possess the comfort of that piece of hindsight as the challenge of potty training our middle son loomed on the horizon.

Our oldest son was a happy-go-lucky kind of

kid from the very beginning. That's one reason that his less than smooth potty training experience caught us off guard. Every other part of his life had been so easy. Even his birth was relatively easy.

That was not the case with our second son, Jonathan. Right out of the starting gate, Jonathan convinced us that brothers are **very** different. Where his older brother had been **easy**, Jonathan seemed determined to be **difficult**. From the beginning, everything seemed to rub Jonathan the wrong way. And to be honest, Jonathan seemed to rub everybody the wrong way. He just couldn't seem to get comfortable with life. As a baby, he fretted and fussed. When he finally started talking, he whined and complained. We were not looking forward to his potty training.

As his second birthday approached, we marked a day on the calendar signifying the official start date for his potty training. We gave ourselves two weeks to summon our courage. Exactly ten days before the chosen day, our plans took an unexpected turn.

On a Saturday afternoon, Kathy and I were sitting on the couch when Jonathan walked into the living room. He was naked from the waist down. All he was wearing was one of those little toddler tee shirts with the adjustable necks. In one hand he was holding a sagging diaper that he had just taken off. In his other hand he held a pair of training pants. To this day we do not know where he found them. In a matter of fact tone, he announced to his mother and me, "I'm not wearing diapers *anymore*. From now on, I'm wearing *men's* pants." With that said, he sat down and stuck his feet carefully through the leg holes of the training pant. Then he stood up and pulled them up snugly. He smiled and nodded his head once as if to say "that takes care of that." Then he turned around and scampered out of the room. Kathy and I stared at each other in stunned silence.

Finally, she managed to ask, "What do you think?"

"I believe we just witnessed a *take charge* attitude," I responded.

In the days that followed, our middle son trained himself. No whining. No crying. No accidents. In the days leading up to his taking matters into his own hands, I decided that he must have had a conversation with himself. It was no doubt influenced by his observing his older brother's trials and tribulations. I imagine that the one-sided conversation must have gone something like this: "These people need some help!"

Two down, one more to go.

Is it not interesting that our children experience their parents as different people in different phases of their lives? During the first two years of our first son's life he encountered two *very* inexperienced parents. We were beginning to feel more comfortable in our role as parents as number two moved through his first years. We were much more laid back by the time number three came on the scene. In the forty-three months that had unfolded between the birth of our first son and the birth of our third son, we had learned a few things. We had asked a lot of questions and discovered some answers. I had even read a little child psychology. In our search for knowledge we had discovered what the *old doctor* said. (Let it be noted that no one has ever quoted what the *young* doctor said.) I could never find out who the old doctor was who was being quoted, but his words were repeated with a sense of awe and respect. They must have come down from Mount Sinai. On the issue of potty training, this is what the *old doctor* said, "I never knew of a child who started to school who didn't know how to go to the bathroom." The wisdom in his words was simple, *take your time.* Our third son, Joseph, would reap the benefits of his parent's growing knowledge.

When the subject of Joseph's potty training came up, Kathy said, "He's all yours."

I had already developed a game plan. This time the operative phrase would be *positive re-enforcement.* The theme for Joseph's potty training experience would be taken from the song titled, *Home on the Range, "where never is heard a discouraging word."* I was determined to become his personal cheerleader. I was fully committed to his success.

On a specified day, I announced to our youngest that we were going to do something *fun.* I led him into the bathroom, stood him in front of the proper facility, pulled his new training pants down to his ankles, and pointed him in the right direction. Then, with enthusiasm in my voice, I cheered, "Let's go Joseph! Let's go Joseph! Show your Daddy what you can do!"

He looked at me like I had lost my mind. He didn't have a **clue**! The days ahead turned out to be most interesting. It's amazing the things that little boys will do when they can't grasp the meaning of your instructions. Standing in **ready** position, Joseph would look out the window, watch a fly on the wall, and look at his toes as he made then wiggle. He smiled a lot. But he wasn't catching on.

Days turned into weeks. We were still making regular trips to the bathroom and going through our routine. I was still cheerleading. All the while he had the cutest bewildered look on his face. He was just not **getting it**. That all changed one afternoon when I arrived home after work.

As a part of my regular routine, I sought him out to check his diaper. After our usual hug and kiss, I ran my index finger down in the front of  his diaper to check for wetness. He was as **dry as a chip.** I quickly called to Kathy, "How long has it been since Joseph's last diaper change?" She appeared in the doorway with a surprised look and exclaimed, "Oh, it's been at least an hour or two!"

I seized the moment! In this business, timing can be **everything**! I grabbed him by the wrist and headed for the bathroom as fast as he could keep up. When we arrived I stood him in place. I left him for a moment and went into action. I quickly turned both sink faucets wide open, and hit the shower control. Then in one motion, I slapped the flush lever as I dropped his pants.

At that **exact** moment, he **sprang a leak**. I cannot say that *I* was taken totally by surprise, but Joseph **was**! With his eyes growing wider and wider, he looked at me as if to say, "well bust my britches!" Again, I seized the moment.

I pounded him on the back and said, "Good boy, Joseph, good boy." Then I hugged him and kissed him and said, "Good boy, Joseph, good boy!" I yelled to his mother, "K-a-t-h-y come in here and see what this boy has done!"

As she rushed into the bathroom, Joseph was standing with his chest thrown out and his mouth wide open. She grabbed him up and hugged him and kissed on him and said, "Good boy, Joseph, good boy." He was soaking it all up! By now his brothers had heard all the commotion and they arrived to give him **high fives**. And of course, they echoed our, "Good boy, Joseph, good boy." I promise you, they capped it off by dancing "ring around the rosey" in the bathroom.

It was quite a celebration, and it made a **big** impression on our youngest.

After that day, whenever he felt the urge, he would announce to anyone who would listen, "Hey, ya'll, I'm **going**," as he headed to the bathroom. Of course, the whole family followed to join in the celebration—at least for the first few days. Then things began to get back to normal. Soon the novelty of Joseph's performances began to wear off. Eventually, he found himself going it alone. Lesson learned.

A few weeks later, I found *myself* alone in the bathroom. As I stood there, minding my own business, I was suddenly shocked by Joseph's chubby little hand pounding on my knee. His face was glowing as he looked up into my eyes and cheered, "Good boy, Daddy, good boy!"

I must admit that I felt *good*. I felt proud of myself, even *motivated*. I was already looking forward to my next trip to the bathroom!

*What a lesson in life from a little boy!*

But, more importantly it drove home for me something that I have always believed. And, it is this: *Life is very much like an echo.* For the most part, what we do and what we say and how we say it has a way of making a return trip. In the end, it all comes down to *sowing* and *reaping*.

# *Chapter 17*

# Asian Eyes

He was one of my best loan customers back in my banking days. I called him Mr. Bhong. I well remember the day when his Dodge Colt cruised onto bank property. I recall the tail pipe dragging the asphalt as he left Broadway and entered the parking lot. The sparks were flying! I must admit that in Trousdale County, Tennessee, his family name does not go back too many generations. He and his wife had come to America shortly after our armed forces left Vietnam. In the early going, communication between this southern boy and my new Vietnamese friend was, shall I say, *interesting*. I was immediately captivated by the courteous manner of the Asian people. When confronted with someone who doesn't speak our language, we southerners just resort to talking louder and *s-l-o-w-e-r*. I even learned to bow graciously in like manner to Mr. Bhong. After a year or two I pretty well had the communication thing **down**.

There was a sense of industriousness about Mr. Bhong that I soon came to admire. I know that he approached repaying a loan with workman-like efficiency. We began our banking relationship when he borrowed a modest sum of money to be paid in monthly installments. He usually "doubled up" on payments, sometimes paying as many as three at one time. As the amount of each loan increased over a period of years, his determination to pay them off ahead of schedule never wavered. His demeanor was always pleasant. I looked forward to seeing him come into the bank.

Eventually, he and his wife decided to trade in their car for a nice late model automobile. You have to admire many immigrants who arrive here. They do understand "delayed gratification." The car for which they traded was by no means new, but it was *new* to them. It was a Dodge Dynasty, silver blue, and it cost $7,200.00. For a purchase of this sum, I requested that Mrs. Bhong co-sign the promissory note. I looked forward to meeting his wife.

Unfortunately, my many conversations with Mr. Bhong had not adequately prepared me for my meeting with Mrs. Bhong. On the appointed day, she entered the bank with their two  daughters. She came straight to my desk in the open lobby and stood—and smiled. I rose from my chair to greet her and according to my previous conditioning I bowed slightly and introduced myself. She returned my bow and smiled a tentative kind of smile. She tried very hard, but could not conceal her uneasiness. I motioned that she take a seat and the girls joined her in a chair close by.

I had decided that the girls' ages were probably 7 and 9 years. As Mrs. Bhong and I continued to talk and bow and smile, I began to notice that the girls' heads were beginning to follow ours. As we bowed, they bowed. I was reminded of one of those dogs that I had seen on the sun deck of cars, the ones whose heads bob up and down when the car hits a bump in the road. You can imagine four heads going up and down in unison.

As I guided Mrs. Bhong through the loan closing, I noticed that the girls were leaning closer and closer toward me. They seemed to find my efforts at communicating with their mother rather entertaining. Occasionally they would look at each other and nod their heads and smile as if some secret kind of communication was going on. I was intrigued by the sheer beauty of these little Asian girls. Their eyes were dark and beautiful as they blinked with wonder and curiosity. Their straight, raven colored hair was so black it took on a blue sheen.

As the loan closing approached its conclusion, I felt compelled to bring these girls into the conversation. By now the older daughter was sitting on the edge of her seat resting her elbows on my desk. I paused, looked into her beautiful, dark Asian eyes and slowly and deliberately asked, "Hon-ey, how are things go-ing in schoo-ool?"

She squinted one eye, shrugged her shoulders, and with a note of resignation in her voice she drawled out, "Ahh, pur-dy gooood."

I was not prepared for her answer! I could not believe it! To use a word from another generation, "I was flabbergasted!" It took me a few seconds to recover. Then it dawned on me! These were southern girls! They were born and bred in the southern United States. We had them talking **normally** from the very beginning!

114

"Pur-dy gooood!" Those words make me think of the pace at which we live. They speak to me of how, in a world marked by constant pressure and accelerated change, it is easy to find ourselves doing a whole bunch of things "pur-dy gooood." at the expense of doing fewer things in an "excellent way." I think of some words my mother would say as I was growing up: "Son, you're burning the candle at both ends," "You're spending yourself too thin," "You've got too many irons in the fire."

So, I pose this question to you: What are the three most important things in your life? Are they receiving most of your time and attention? Are you doing "purdy good?" Is there time or room for excellence in your life?

I've heard it said that there are two distinct phases in one's life. One is the time when "you could if you would, but you didn't." The second is the time when "you would if you could, but you can't." May we never forget that the clock is ticking.

# *Chapter 18*

# The Sharecropper

On a cold and dreary winter's day I went to see an old friend for what would be the last time. The clouds were low and grey and spitting snow as I took the gravel country road that meandered through the countryside until it ended in front of the white farmhouse. Mr. Marvin was a sharecropper. He had never achieved the American dream of owning his own home. All his working life, he earned the roof over his head by giving up a share of each year's crop to the landowner.

I had known him all of my life. Having attended the same country church, I had seen him every Sunday since I could remember. He was a big man whose belly jiggled when he laughed or coughed. He smoked Pall Mall cigarettes and could make a cigarette stick to his lower lip. As a boy, I took special delight in watching the end of his lit cigarette jump up and down when he talked. That was intriguing to a little boy.

I must interject here that Mr. Marvin loved hot dogs. I would say that he considered them to be  a luxury. At all day singings and dinner on the ground, someone always brought hot dogs and Mr. Marvin would always find them. At these special summer events, I would take it upon myself to investigate with amusement as to

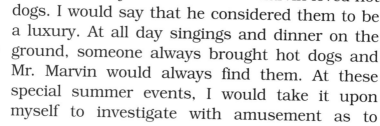

whether or not he had discovered the hot dog platter. It never failed. He would always have two on his plate. As the years went by, the women of the church conspired to make certain that someone furnished hot dogs. It was a most subtle act of kindness. *Everyone* loved Mr. Marvin.

His voice was unmistakable, heavily influenced by a humble life and a 4th grade education. His prayers were a special treat. Each prayer invariably showcased two phrases from which he never deviated. "And Lord, I would not fail to thank you for that day down in the old cow lot when you spoke peace to my troubled soul." That was my favorite.

Then, there was, "And Lord, when you are done with us on this low ground of sin and sorrow, and we've stacked the working tools of life, receive us into that upper and better kingdom in a world that has no end and we'll be careful to give you all the praise, in Jesus name. Amen."

Mr. Marvin drove a 1957 Chevy. It was a turquoise and white two-tone, BelAir model. It had to have been at least ten years old when he bought it. In the late 1970s, he traded up to a '64 Impala.

Years later when I became a banker and reviewed multiple financial statements, I sometimes wondered what his financial statement would have looked like. Had he ever moved, I suspect that all of his "earthly possessions" would have fit nicely in the back of a pick-up truck.

As I arrived that December day, I left my car and headed for the back of the house. These were country people. Their front door was rarely, if ever, used. Approaching the screened-in back porch, I noticed that plastic had been stretched over the screening and tacked neatly around the edges for the winter. Mr. Marvin's wife, "Miss" Beatrice, meek as a mouse, met me at the back steps. She was a little woman of fair complexion whose slightness of build bordered on frailty. With her usual quiet shyness, she whispered, "Come on in." I followed her through a small room filled with all the delicious aromas of a country kitchen—simmering onions, chicken broth, and corn bread.

As we came to the living room, she pushed the door open and I stepped inside. When I entered the room, I was taken back by two things. First, the room was uncomfortably warm, almost to the point of taking one's breath, and second, the room had a uniquely human scent about it. It was not offensive. It was a combination of the smells of earth and smoke and sweat and wood and leather and medications. The combination was strangely comforting, almost as if to beckon, "Real people live here. Come on in."

With a weak hand, Mr. Marvin motioned for me to join him as he sat before a steadily burning fire fueled by lumps of coal in the fireplace. We sat in rickety rocking chairs whose arms almost touched and spent the better part of the afternoon in unhurried conversation—mostly about life.

The subject eventually changed to his imminent death. He said, "Jack, you know when the doctors found my cancer they only gave me six months to live." I answered, "Yes, sir." Then through tired eyes that had taken on a triumphant gleam he said, "You know it's been over a year." I answered, "Yes, sir" again. Then he said, "The Lord has given me twice the time that the doctors' said I had, so I'm not asking for anymore time. All I'm asking for in the time that I have left is that He will just let me help somebody."

I promise you at that very moment I had the presence of mind to fully take in the essence of what was going on. I found myself climbing into a tiny mental helicopter and flying to the furthest corner of the room at ceiling level and looking back down on this scene of which I was a part. In my mind's eye, I can still recall every detail of that which I saw. I was witnessing a man who had stepped outside *himself*. Here was a dying man who was looking past his approaching death and seeking to help someone else.

From my observation point I was careful to allow the emotions of the moment to wash over me again and again. I wanted never to forget my time in his presence.

He had no idea that day that I would be one of the answers to his prayer. Nor could he have known that I would someday share his act of selflessness with thousands of people, that his influence would live far beyond the room of his simple farmhouse through me.

119

Phillips Brooks said, "Greatness after all, in spite of its name, appears to be not so much a certain size and a certain quality in human lives. It may be present in lives whose range is very small."

# Chapter 19

# Granny Lena and the Little Horse

It was one of those spring evenings when the bottom falls out of the sky, crashing thunder, spectacular displays of lightning and driving rainfall, one of nature's ways of reminding us that we are not really in control of anything. The setting was Sunday evening church in the country. The storm had whipped in out of nowhere. The rain came in sheets. Against the church's tin roof, the sound was deafening.

As the church service came to a close, the rain was unrelenting. Conversations focused on the rising water in the creeks that some would have to ford on their way back home. My mother was six years old. Her mother, my Granny Lena, would have to take their horse drawn buggy across the widest creek. Some speculated that the floodwaters would be out of the creek banks soon, if not already. Others insisted that my grandmother stay overnight with them until the  waters went down. Granny Lena, however, had made up her mind. She would take her chances. "Neither hail, nor (in this case) high water," would stop her.

As they made a mad dash for the horse and buggy tied up under the trees at the edge of the church yard, they felt the full fury of the rain. After a few frantic moments of getting the horse loose and turning the buggy around, horse, buggy, and passengers were off into the night. By now they were as wet as drowned rats. As the storm continued to bear down on them, Granny Lena drove the buggy with intensity and resolve. As they rode into the night, the driving rain blow directly into their faces.

Granny Lena, undaunted by the storm, stood up in the buggy and leaned forward as she continued to lay on the whip. Amid the whipping, she yelled and called on the horse. All the while, my mother was thinking about the creek and just how high the water would be.

Suddenly, the creek was upon them, the flash flood waters thrashing wildly as it crashed past the point where the road ended at water's edge. They could hear the water before they saw it. The  little horse hesitated as they reached the top of the creek bank. Then he came to a complete halt. Granny Lena seemed to lose all sanity as she began to scream and apply the horse whip with renewed vengeance. The little horse, seemingly oblivious to the weight of the leather, proceeded cautiously down to the rising water. Then he stopped again.

My mother's six-year-old heart was pounding so hard in her throat that she could not swallow. Granny Lena was not going to turn around. She continued to whip the little horse urging him forward. The little horse took one step out into the churning current, which struck him just above the knee. Then, strangely, he twisted his hoof as though screwing it down to feel solid footing. He shifted his weight before taking the next step. He took another step and shifted his weight again.

The rain's relentless pelting burned my mother's skin as the flashes of lightning revealed the grotesque silhouettes of the trees, leaf and limb flouncing wildly at the mercy of the wind. The rising water was now crashing against the running board of the buggy and all the while Granny Lena was screaming, now sounding like a banshee. The scene was one of heightened 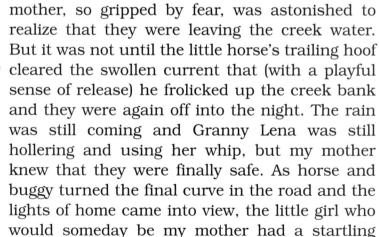 chaos, and at the center of the storm's eye in what seemed like a world away was the brave little horse taking one step at a time, checking his footing and shifting his weight; so focused on his mission that he seemed oblivious to the goings on around him.

Time and eternity passed in slow motion. Suddenly, they were at the other side. My mother, so gripped by fear, was astonished to realize that they were leaving the creek water.  But it was not until the little horse's trailing hoof cleared the swollen current that (with a playful sense of release) he frolicked up the creek bank and they were again off into the night. The rain was still coming and Granny Lena was still hollering and using her whip, but my mother knew that they were finally safe. As horse and buggy turned the final curve in the road and the lights of home came into view, the little girl who would someday be my mother had a startling revelation: "On that unforgettable night so many years ago, that little horse had a whole lot more sense than my mama did."

Some would call it horse sense. Others might call it **common** sense. But, there is something to be said for the ability to remain calm under fire. A generation ago people talked comfortably about an anchor for the soul, a changeless center that allows one to proceed undaunted by events.

Could it be possible that our Creator gave the little horse, through instinct, that which humanity has passed up by choice?

# Chapter 20

# Epilogue:
# On a Spring Morning

Not too many years ago on a spring morning, I was aroused from a deep sleep just at the break of dawn. I am not an early riser, but on this day, I sat up in bed and turned and dropped my feet on the floor. I was in full view of the bedroom window that faced the east. The morning sky, just ahead of the rising sun, was splashed with splendid variations of purples and oranges. A chance to capture **this** sunrise was just too tantalizing to pass up. I felt strangely drawn to go outside and take it in.

I found my way through the still, darkened house. I opened the front door and stepped out into the morning air. The morning stillness had the hush of dawn about it. Only a few early birds could be heard chirping quietly nearby. The air was heavy with the coming of morning. The sun would be showing its face at any moment.

Then, far into the distance, the morning silence was broken by the faint howling and yapping of a family of coyotes. It was a sound that they only make when arriving back at their den after a night of hunting. Their banter only lasted for a few seconds and then all was quiet again.

At that moment, from the edge of the woods a quarter mile away, I heard the shadowy "whoo—

whoo—whoo,whoo,whoo" of a great horned owl as he bid the night farewell.

To my far right on the farm across the road I heard the deep lowing of a mamma cow. In a moment she called again. I knew that she was headed in search of her calf that she had hidden the night before. Now, she was on the move. Deep and low she called. On she went lowing quietly.

Then to my far left, I heard her calf, not too many days from newborn, answer. His first call was almost as weak as the bleat of a kid goat. She responded. Her lowing now had an urgency about it. She was picking up her pace. The location of her baby was now exposed. He answered again, this time more strongly. He had recognized his mama's voice. She is now in a trot. Mama cow calling, baby answering. Suddenly, all was quiet. They are reunited. All is as it should be.

Through my mind's eye, I could see her calf in the days ahead, his tail high in the air, his back arched as he sidled up to his mother for his next meal. And, I could see him as he dropped his  chin to the ground and slammed his head upward into the bottom of her udder emphatically letting her know that it was time to let her ivory nectar flow. I, too, could see him standing in a dreamlike daze when he was finished, his mouth encircled with frothy foam. He would be full, his mother content—until the next time. My mind picture was interrupted by the next sound of the morning.

The sun was just showing its face when, in the distance, a friendly pack of dogs barked happily as they welcomed the morning. I sensed that something magical was going on. From a pin oak time in the front yard a mourning dove cooed softly. By now, the birds of spring began to come alive with all the melodies of springtime. I found myself reveling in this rapturous symphony of sounds.

The sun was rising faster now and the sky was ablaze. From a far away pasture, a seasoned herd sire trumpeted a challenge and a warning to all comers. That which started out as a deep bellow ended in a shrill whistle. All to let any doubters know that *he* was the bull of *these* woods!

The sun, having let go of the horizon, was now in full view. That is when I heard it, the unmistakable "Er, er, err, ERRRR!" of a proud barnyard rooster, as if to say, "It's not morning until I say it's morning!"

As if that were not enough, a nervous quail, called out a familiar, "Bob white" from a pasture nearby. It was almost too much to take in—so many of God's creatures stepping out on the stage of the morning in such a small window of time. It was, indeed, magical.

I paused for a moment to let it all soak in. I knew that it would never happen *exactly* this way again.

In the great scheme of life there are a few moments when I have experienced a *oneness* with it all, the wonder of creation, the rhythm of the seasons, the circle of life. As I considered all of that on that glorious morning, the words of an old John Denver song came into my head, "Thank God, I'm a country boy."